She Couldn't Spell Debt

She Couldn't Spell Debt

Consuelo Danita

Publisher: Consuelo Danita

ISBN: 978-0-9994926-2-8 Paperback

Library of Congress Control Number: 2017916210

Dedication

To Felipe, Craig, Tiffany, Jody, Lora, Ashley, Ronaldo, Doreen, Mario, Dr. Mark Sayeg and Ms. Tina.

Thank you for the beautiful gift of encouragement.

Contents

Chapter 1: Her Enemy

No! No! No! I don't want to be here, and I am getting out of this class at once!" That is what Callie told her accounting teacher. The teacher calmly replied, "Callie, you have not given it a chance and why are you so irritated?" "I don't want to give it a chance and I am not irritated. I am going to speak to my counselor and withdraw from this class." When Callie left the class, she walked as if she were taking part in a fast-walking race, holding her head up high while swinging her hips and arms like they could become dislocated at any moment.

Although Callie said she was not irritated when she visited her counselor's office, she was furious and said, "My accounting teacher is forcing me to stay in a class that I do not like and where I do not want to be. Furthermore, what do I need accounting for?" Because it was Callie's first day in class, the counselor was puzzled by her feelings. What made her snap? Would she really get the truth from Callie or was it that Callie was a spoiled teen and if she did not want to do something, she would not do it?

Her counselor skillfully found the underlying cause of the situation within ten minutes. She learned that Callie was afraid of math. She barely passed algebra and she hated geometry. Once Callie's counselor understood the problem, she said, "You will need this in life." Callie decided to stand her ground and was annoyed that she was not getting her way. Her counselor said, "I am sending you back to class. Although you are concerned about failing this class, you will not fail, only succeed. I will not let you quit. I will check with your teacher and monitor your progress."

As hurriedly as Callie had walked to her counselor's office was the same way she returned to class. She grabbed her books and went to a vacant desk in the last row to sulk. If Callie's classmates had not intervened, she would have gone home. They said, "We do not know about accounting either; so, we can help each other." As time went by, Callie saw that her counselor was right. This was a different type of math and surprisingly she came to enjoy accounting. Her grades were quite good, and her friends' grades were good.

Not knowing what she would study in college, Callie decided to study what her friends studied, accounting. Little did she know that within a few years her life would change drastically, and she would really need to use what she learned in accounting. She would certainly need to know how to budget and how to spend, especially when times were hard.

Over and over, she was told that money will not make you happy; still, she was unhappy when she did not have it. She concluded that happiness had to be connected to money. Her attitude about money was partially correct because she learned that money served as a protection, just like having godly wisdom served as a protection. But it was the unbalanced love of money that could twist your judgment. Since Callie did not always have enough money, to a degree, it proved to be more beneficial than the outcome she had initially envisioned for herself.

Without a doubt, she had envisioned financial security, never ever having to worry about money. Certainly, by observing some people, she learned that money could mask who you really are or change who you were. Financial security caused some individuals who were not prepared for success, to develop negative characteristics like haughtiness and presumptuousness, characteristics which could indisputably affect relationships with friends, family and acquaintances. Instead of experiencing financial security though, Callie experienced intermittent debt.

Sure, at times she did not have a problem with debt. After a while, debt chased her down like a cheetah running down a deer. Having debt produced destructive traits in her more than ever, especially negativity. Her negative thoughts about herself contributed to her low self-esteem. She made jokes about herself that were demoralizing. Fortunately, in time, she could keep the destructive behavior under control. The destructive behavior? Callie really did not know her behavior was destructive. She thought it was just having fun and taking a break from her problems. How could drinking a cocktail here and there be destructive? Well it was. Because her one drink was equivalent to four for a normal person. During an evening, she would consume several, let's say "four for one" drinks.

Since she did not recognize that the drinking was destructive, she would take others with her to the "four for one" fun evening. Only one person made a comment that caused Callie to re-evaluate what she considered fun and harmless as destructive. Here is the comment that Pierre, her future husband, said, "Callie, it is not normal to have that many drinks in one sitting. Actually, it's not ladylike."

Ouch! That really stung her. She considered herself a lady, a southern lady, and that one comment got her attention. Later, she mentioned to her momma what Pierre said to her. Her momma said, "Callie, I thought you may have had a problem." "Momma!" she said excitedly. "Why didn't you say something?" Maria said, "Well, Callie I just thought you were having a problem with your boyfriend."

Pierre went further to challenge Callie. He said, "If you in fact do not have a problem with alcohol, stop drinking for one month." She took the challenge and stopped. After one-month Callie laughed and said, "Ok. I did it. Let's go out to celebrate."

Unquestionably, she made some very bad decisions. Yet, the irony of experiencing debt forced her to examine herself and her actions more closely. This led Callie to the conclusion that she, not someone else, had made some bad decisions. She had to accept that she was deficient or imperfect in her judgment, since she readily strived for perfection. She had no reason to point the finger at anyone.

Callie also developed some positive qualities because of having debt. She needed positive qualities like humility, empathy and mercy, to name just a few to become more dominant in her personality. The outcome of not experiencing financial security was for sure more beneficial to her, especially since she needed a fuller measure of those helpful qualities.

Callie was humbled when she recognized that there were some things beyond her control. To help her cope, Callie started living by her new-found motto: "I cannot be the general manager of the universe." She learned to be more empathetic toward others, especially when she remembered that she had been in similar situations. She learned that she could not always get her way. When she was in a financial position to extend loans, she showed mercy when the borrower was unable to repay the loan, at times forgiving the debt.

Remembering the advice an elderly friend gave her, helped Callie to forgive the debt without reprimand. Her elderly rich friend once said, "I don't give loans to friends. If I cannot afford to give them the money they need, I just say I don't have it." She went on to say, "Giving a loan to a friend for a business venture is quite different from giving a loan to a friend who is in dire need and really cannot afford to repay it. If you are going to extend a loan to friends, just make sure that you are financially able to lose it. Don't expect repayment in some cases. Don't charge a friend to help them out." By applying her elderly friend's counsel, Callie could keep relationships peaceful.

However, at nine years old, while in elementary school, Callie was introduced to an enemy that appeared harmless; but, advanced to being brutal. It began with one word and that word came from her very first spelling bee.

She was excited about the spelling bee. No doubt it was because in her heart, she had a desire to perform before others. Maria worked diligently with Callie in preparation for the contest; although Callie was confident about her ability to spell and pronounce words correctly. So much so, she would gently correct her momma on the pronunciation of several words. Maria would humbly say, "Callie, I thought that you pronounce the word this way." Callie would respond, "No momma, this is how you pronounce this word." Since she accepted what Callie said, Maria would just let it go.

Callie was progressing well and the big day for the spelling bee was finally about to take place in the school gymnasium where only four children would qualify to go to the state finals. The kids were eliminated one by one. Some could not utter a sound, and some would simply misspell a one or two syllable word. It was nerve racking and exhilarating at the same time for her, making the palms of her hands switch between hot and sweaty or cold and trembling.

Callie remembered looking at the different kids misspelling words that she thought were ever so easy to spell. In her condescending mind, she would say, "What is wrong with them?" Her best friend at school, Danielle, misspelled Britain and of course she was eliminated early in the competition. Wow! To Callie, Danielle appeared smart. In fact, her entire family was extremely smart. Well at that point, Callie felt that this was just unbelievable, downright ridiculous!

The spelling bee continued for a while, and it was down to five people standing after several rounds had occurred. The teacher called out "debt" and it was Callie's turn. Callie wondered if she should ask, "Do you mean debbed?" That's how she used to pronounce it. It seemed like an eternity. She was sick to her stomach, and she was now like her fellow classmates, speechless. So, what would she do?

She remembered that word clearly because her momma, Maria, had discussed this word in detail with her. Still, she did not ask any questions after the word was called out. In any case, after having this seemingly long silent conversation with herself, she spelled the word "debt" as "d-e-h-t." The teacher said, "That is incorrect." Callie had mixed up the conversation in her head. Many times, she questioned her momma about the pronunciation. It was a four-letter word and one syllable.

If she had not been so consumed with correcting her momma, she would have remembered that d-e-h-t was how she spelled the word, not how the book presented it. If she had such an uncertainty about the word, why didn't she ask a teacher the correct pronunciation? Could it be for this reason? She was a child that thought she knew more than her momma and her teacher knew.

Callie felt like she was going to throw up. The fifth person to be eliminated was Callie, leaving the four winners. She would not be going to the state finals. Her friends that had been eliminated earlier from the competition surrounded her after the competition, trying to find out what had occurred. With tears rolling down her cheeks, she told them, "I couldn't spell debt."

She was hurt and angry. You may wonder how could one little girl express those two emotions at one time? She had experience from the time she was three years old. Her momma said when she felt unhappy or angry, she would hold her breath until she turned blue.

Later, Callie asked her momma: "Why didn't I believe that you had pronounced the word correctly? Her momma responded, "Because I had a tie-tongue." Translating that, Maria meant that she had a slight speech impediment. There were just some words that Maria simply could not pronounce.

The irony of the whole thing is that Maria was an avid reader who loved to read mystery novels and because she devoured books, Callie's daddy said to Maria, "I bought you a set of encyclopedias because you like to read so much. Maybe that will hold you for a while." Undeniably, Maria was no dummy. She was smart, and she expressed that her little girl was smart. On the other hand, Callie was foolish to belittle Maria's knowledge of words because she could not say them properly.

At that spelling bee, Callie had just received a wakeup call. There is always someone bigger and better or smarter and wiser. At that moment, she hated the word debt. Nevertheless, this was a superficial blow for Callie compared to how that word would prove to have a profound meaning later in life.

Chapter 2: Did Heritage Matter?

Callie was born in the deep south in a small town located thirty miles from a main road. There was only one way into the town and only one way out of the town. Speaking of oneness, it was primarily one of everything in the town which included one movie theatre, one gas station, one juke-joint, one hospital, one doctor's office, one high school, one elementary school, one radio station, one judge, one lawyer and they were brothers.

Many things simply did not exist that she could remember. There were no fine dining restaurants, no fast-food restaurants, no museums, no aquariums, no television stations, and no zoos, except the people who acted like animals.

Callie's family was well-known in the community to say the least. Her granddaddy, Louie Clausell, did not know that he had instilled a longing in his granddaughter at a very young age. His opinion that she was smart and would do better in a larger city developed into her goal which eventually took her away from the small, southern town of Monroeville.

To cope with small town living, Callie developed a unique sense of humor along with a far-reaching imagination. Unlike many of the citizens and relatives who appreciated small town living, Callie, on the other hand, wanted to experience city living and was ready to go.

Her granddaddy, who was of French descent, said to her in a deep southern New Orleans sort of dialect, "Gurl, I toll yo momma and daddy when you wuz bout three yeahs old that you wuz too smart to be in dis heah town. Yawl needs to take that gurl to da city." Whatever he saw in her,

Callie could not tell you, other than she could not let him down or herself for that matter.

Her daddy's side of the family took pride in their heritage. She paid little attention to it. How many families have been able to trace their family back to the late 1700's? Callie's father's side of the family could, and this is what granddaddy Louie told her: "My granddaddy's daddy wuz da son of a soldier fur Napolyun who wuz over dare in France. My greet granddaddy left France to come to da South. And he came down dare in Mobile and started farming." Callie asked her granddaddy a question and he said, "Gurl just let me tell ya da story fore ya ask me any mo questions, cuz I know how ya is." "Ok, granddaddy."

"He went back and foth to France. When he came one time, he married a gurl from heah, nair Virginyah. He left his wife and chillen in Mobile and when he came back, sumpen had hapen to all of em, except my granddaddy. Ret after dat, my granddaddy's daddy died, and so my granddaddy went back to France to git what his daddy left em."

Callie said, "Ok granddaddy, that's enough. I do not really like history. So, I do not want to know any more right now." Granddaddy Louie laughed: "Ok gurl. That's enuf fur taday."

Although Callie did not fully know the story of her heritage until adulthood, her unverifiable knowledge of her great great granddaddy's example of purchasing land impressed upon her the value of making sound purchases, purchases that would bring dividends as well as provide an inheritance for family.

What Callie thought was unverifiable gossip, now was about to change to verifiable facts. One of her cousins decided to educate her about the Clausell family using documents he had received from family members who had diligently performed detailed research.

Do you think Callie was impressed? She was not impressed because she did not read it. After years of keeping it in a file, she mentioned it to an older friend who asked to read it. After the friend read for hours at Callie's house, the friend took it home and read every bit of it. She called Callie to let her know she was returning the documents and the friend demanded that Callie read it.

Callie finally read bits and pieces because the information load was just overwhelming. Here is a summary of what Callie read, which was close to what her granddaddy Louie was trying to tell her. Granddaddy Louie's great granddaddy was Count Bertrand Clausell. Count Clausell was born in Mirepoix, Ariège, France on December 12, 1773 and died in Chateau Lecurien on April 21, 1842.

In 1789, he married Susan from Virginia. They returned to France where he joined Napoleon as his foreign minister and progressed to General. Napoleon sent him to Haiti with General Le Clere to beat the African General Christoffel in Haiti. Count Bertrand Clausell took his family with him. The Carib Indians in Haiti had a good relationship with the French and a family from Haiti looked after Count Bertrand Clausell's family for a while. In 1803, when it seemed like the army of France was going to lose, Callie's great great great granddaddy Bertrand took his wife and five sons to Mobile after which he returned to France to fight.

After Napoleon was defeated and King Louis XVIII regained power, Count Bertrand Clausell was stripped of his title, and he was sentenced to death. He escaped to the United States in early 1816. He settled in the Mobile Bay area and began farming and writing his espose. After a while, he returned to France.

When he returned to Mobile, he discovered that his wife had died. Two of his sons were killed while fighting for Stonewall Jackson. Two sons had gone West. Only Thomas, his fifth son was in Mobile. He was living with his mother's housekeeper.

Sad news did not stop there. Count Bertrand Clausell's daddy died, and he again returned to France to claim his inheritance. The Count left his only surviving 18-year-old son, Thomas, with a letter of credit if he needed it. He didn't need it because he had begun an extremely profitable business, breeding children for the slave trade. It was short lived, and Thomas closed the farm. He did not have to use the letter of credit because tragic news presented another source of income for Thomas. Count Bertrand Clausell died, and Thomas was the only heir. Thomas left for France.

After receiving his inheritance, Thomas returned to South Alabama where he bought six sections of land that had six hundred and forty acres in each section making a total of 3,840 acres in 1842 from the state of Alabama between $1.20 to $2.00 per acre in Monroeville. Basically, this amounted to about one third of Monroeville.

Eventually, Thomas returned to visit the Carib Indians his family had befriended in Haiti. The daddy of the family insisted that Callie's great great granddaddy Thomas bring Lucinda to America to give her a good start. When he returned to Monroeville in 1856, he brought back the Carib girl named Lucinda.

They never married; but she had four children for him. The children were given his last name and one section of land was given to each of his three sons – Nelson, Billy and Stephen. Billy was granddaddy Louie's daddy. After Callie's great great granddaddy Thomas died, Lucinda gave Martha, their only daughter, the section of land with the main house. Afterward, Sections I, II, III, IV were deeded: "Forever Clausell."

Callie was not one to hold grudges against someone, especially if she did not know all the facts. And this principle applied to her great great granddaddy. But what she knew about her great great granddaddy was that he set a good example of purchasing land that would bring dividends to him as well as provide an inheritance for his family. She was impressed by his business shrewdness. And she wondered if she could ever achieve what he had accomplished.

Callie spent a lot of time with her granddaddy when she was younger. One question plagued her tremendously. So, she asked, "Granddaddy, why do the kids think that we are rich? I cain't tell that we have a lot of money or rich like the kids say." He replied, "Of my daddy's three broders, my daddy gave his potion to da udder broders."

She didn't know what he meant. She wasn't sure if he meant land, money or something else. He went on to say, "There wuz a disagreement. My daddy did not want to have anythang to do wit it!" To her, the dispute must have been about money, since she had asked her granddaddy why the kids thought that the Clausell family was rich.

Callie knew that the Clausell family-owned lots of property. She guessed since most of the area was named after her family, the kids assumed that they were rich. After her granddaddy told her that story, she felt that there were some similarities between her and her great granddaddy. She hated conflict. She hated fussing. She hated fighting. She would rather be the loser, so to speak, to preserve peace. She did not want to argue or be at odds with people. That thinking was like a doubled edge sword. It could be favorable and unfavorable simultaneously. Her great granddaddy wanted to keep peace; however, in doing that, he had to make a sacrifice. It appears it was a financial sacrifice. It would prove to be the same for Callie.

She learned a lot about her granddaddy too. He was her favorite relative and she always liked being around him. He was a calm, delightful person who she never saw expressing any sort of anger toward her or anyone else for that matter. She never saw a frown or dent in his face, showing even the slightest bit of displeasure. He did not yell because he was a smooth southern French man. He rarely meddled in anyone's business, even his children from what she could tell. She took after him. Although, he did not do the things that some may have thought were memorable, they were memorable to her. For instance, he took her to get her driver's license when her parents were working. She approached her granddaddy while he was sitting in his car in her Aunt's yard: "Granddaddy, I want to get my driver's license. Can you help me? Will you take me? Momma and daddy are working." He asked a few questions and concluded with, "Yep, I'll take ya."

Another memorable gesture from her granddaddy came about when her teacher was pressuring her to sew an outfit for her home economics class. The teacher said, "Your sister has taken home economics every year. And she has learned to sew. You are a senior and have not learned to sew." Callie said, "I can sew. I have been sewing for a long time since I was in the fourth grade. I made a skirt that I won an award for in a girls' club."

Clearly, the teacher did not believe Callie. She said, "If that is true, make a pantsuit for class." Callie told her momma about the conversation and the challenge she accepted from her teacher. Her momma said, "Ok. Go ask your granddaddy for some money." Maria had an air of sarcasm behind the comment. Callie ignored that and ran down the road to his house. She was excited to tell her granddaddy what took place at school.

He asked, "How much money do ya need gurl?" She answered, "About ten dollars." He gave her the money to buy the mint green fabric and other necessities for the pantsuit project. Callie completed that project like she was a professional seamstress. Her teacher was impressed because Callie worked on it without any help from the teacher.

Another memorable time with her granddaddy was when he showed her how to eat raw oysters. He would laugh when she would cringe trying to eat them. They would sit in the kitchen at the table with this big container of slimy oysters. He would say, "Heah gurl, put some hot sauce on it." She would say, "Granddaddy, how in the world can you eat that? That's just plain nasty." Was that memorable to her? Yes, indeed.

His wife, grandma Liz, is what the children called her. She never worked outside of the home. She loved to cook, and she cooked well. Her favorite dessert to make was Mississippi Mud pie. It took her the longest time to cook one thing. But, oh boy when she finished cooking, it was good. Callie never remembered her cooking a lot of dishes at one time. Her grandma would always have peas and okra, or okra and collards. Or she would prepare cornbread with one big pot of gumbo or jambalaya. She'd say, "Go in the kitchen. There is some food in there if you want it." She was very particular about her house. She kept it clean. Callie used to laugh at her when she complained about her granddaddy coming into the house to use her "good towels" to bathe. Her grandma hated the grease, dirt and grime. She was always fussing at him about something. It amazed Callie so much how her granddaddy never let it bother him for as long as she could remember. He just had a natural smile on his face. It was as if he did not have a care in the world.

They were married over seventy years when her granddaddy died. Grandma Liz died the following year. Callie's granddaddy Louie was born in 1909 as the youngest of eleven children. The sister that he loved to have fun with was born in 1896. He married grandma Liz in 1924 when he was fifteen years old. She was thirteen.

Callie told her husband that her granddaddy had a nonchalant attitude. As Pierre grew to understand Callie

23

better, he would say, "You are like granddaddy Louie." She was never offended by his remark. She loved granddaddy Louie. To her, it was a compliment.

Pierre asked Callie's granddaddy why he didn't own livestock. Her granddaddy said, "Son, I don't want anythang live." Pierre was tickled by his statement and would often say out of the clear blue sky, "Callie, I am like granddaddy Louie. I do not want anything live."

When granddaddy Louie said that he did not want anything live, it taught Callie to think things all the way through. Having something "live" was much more demanding than he was willing to commit to personally. Possibly, he had experienced the demands of having animals before or he had learned it from observing others. No doubt, having farm animals would come at a price and he had calculated the cost: Too much work. In either case, that was enough for Callie to see and learn from his statement: "I don't want anythang live."

About dusk dark when Callie's cousin from New Orleans and Callie were headed down to granddaddy Louie's house, her cousin noticed something move on the side of the road. He addressed Callie by her nickname that he had given her: "Moon, did you see that? What was that?" She replied, "It's a possum, I think." He was so excited. He pulled over to the side of the road, jumped out, went to his trunk and pulled out a tool. Callie started yelling, "What are you going to do with that?" He said, "Callie I am going to get that possum for granddaddy."

They were headed to their granddaddy's house because Callie's cousin had a gift for him. Now the cousin just wanted to give him something that he enjoyed eating. Well, he went into the woods not far from the roadside and got the animal. She was terribly upset. He said, "Don't worry Moon. It's dead." He put it in his trunk. Within about two minutes they were at their granddaddy's house. They walked in and exchanged greetings. Her cousin gave their granddaddy the wrapped gift he had brought with him. As they were leaving, he told their granddaddy, "Oh, granddaddy, I left something else in the truck for you. They left for the party.

The next morning when they entered their granddaddy's house, the granddaddy, addressed Callie's cousin: "You put a possum in my truck and dat possum tow

25

the inside of my truck up trying ta git outta deah." "Come on granddaddy, I actually thought it was dead." Granddaddy Louie said, "Son, no it wuz live!" Callie laughed so hard. True to the possum's nature, it had played dead. Her cousin's gift had turned into their granddaddy's expense; yet he was not angry.

Since Callie's Granddaddy lived a calm and quiet life, minding his own business, this was the life Callie would strive for, minding her own business. Not that she did not care about others, she just felt that it was right to let people live their life and make their personal decisions, the same courtesy that she wanted to have extended to her.

An incident that Granddaddy Louie shared with Callie made her granddaddy cry and she had never seen her granddaddy cry. When he was a young man, he drove his daddy to town. Her great granddaddy wanted to go to a hardware store. When granddaddy Louie parked the car, and walked with his daddy to the store, the owner said to her great granddaddy, you can come in, not him, alluding to granddaddy Louie.

The tears rolled down her granddaddy's cheeks as he recounted the story. She asked why he was not allowed to go into the store. He said, "Because gurl I had engine in me." Dealing with rejection or prejudice can have the same feeling as dealing with debt. Both to Callie were just plain awful.

Then she thought, granddaddy always talked about his daddy, who died one year before Callie was born. It never dawned on her to ask about his momma. She just never thought about it. Can you believe that? That is just pure crazy. That same day, she asked why he had never talked about his momma. For a second time, with a pitiful face he said, "Because she wuz mean, and she wuz mean to all of us chillen." Then with a great intensity he exclaimed, "Gurl, I didn't like hur! Nobody did!"

Callie pleaded with him to describe her more vividly. She wanted to know more of what no one talked about. She wanted to know what her great grandmomma looked like. He sighed, "Well, she wudn't more than ninety-eight pounds soaking wet. She had pretty coal black wavy hair. She was dark – black like midnight. Her hair was straight as an arrow, not a cul anywhere. When she looked at us chillen hard, all of us knew, better start running. Gurl she was quiet too when she sneaked up on ya."

That was Callie's first introduction to her great grandmomma by granddaddy Louie. Callie wondered if his skin color mattered to his momma because her granddaddy had lightly tanned olive skin with green eyes. Most of his siblings had his skin coloring or lighter with green eyes. Not one of her children was dark skinned.

It seemed like hatred abounded in the small town of Monroeville. Callie's momma told her of an incident that had arisen when she was fourteen years old. Callie's grandmomma was a maid. She worked for a family that regularly vacationed at their cottage on the beach about ninety miles from Monroeville and she normally went with the family on their summer trips. Callie never knew her granddaddy on her momma's side of the family. He had died before Callie was born.

Her momma Maxine, as she unenthusiastically called her, was now a single parent with ten children. A few had left home. This time Momma Maxine did not want to go with the family who she worked for regularly. She sent Callie's Momma in her place.

Maybe, the norm in that day was to send a child to work for the parent. Momma Maxine knew that as a single parent, she needed every bit of money she could get to take care of her family financially. Just imagine what losing that income would have done. Being a single parent with many responsibilities which included giving emotionally and financially for her family was like a small business owner that had to do everything. There were no breaks or hardly any downtime. Maybe, Momma Maxine, a forty-six-year-old single parent, just needed some down time.

When Callie's Momma and her employer, Miss Peters, arrived at the cottage on the beach, Miss Peters gave her instructions as to what should occur that day. Maria would be in different housing further down from where they were staying. Miss Peters said, "Maria, if it rains, please do not come back up to the house as we probably will not go swimming. If it does not rain, please come back to the house, but only at dinner time." Miss Peters continued, "You can go down to your room now."

She went to her housing and went to sleep. Suddenly, there was a loud knock on the window. One of the children hollered, "They want you to come back up to the house." "Why? It's raining." The child said, "I don't know why. They just want you back up at the house." Reluctantly, Maria went.

When she got there, the son-in-law of Miss Peters reprimanded her. He asked her, "Why were you down in your room?" She responded, "Miss Peters told me to go down there and to only come back to the cottage if it did not rain, and that was to be at dinner time." He said, "You are lying." "No, I am not lying. Where is Miss Peters? She will tell you the truth." The son-in-law responded, "She's at the other house." Maria uttered, "I am going to get her. She'll tell you." Miss Peters son-in-law said, "You are not going anywhere." "Yes, I am" Maria announced. "Girl, I ought to slap you for talking back to me." She said, "If you do, you will get slapped." When Maria told Callie that story, Callie got chills up and down her spine. For a child to speak that way to an older person was disrespectful. Just add the prejudice factor that existed. Certainly, this was suicidal in the early fifties in the deep south.

Callie interrupted Maria, "Did you really say that?" She said, "Yes, Callie I did!" "Momma, were you really going to hit him?" She said, "Yes Callie. I was going to hit him." "What happened?" "He drew his hand back to hit me and his wife caught it." Jack's wife said, "Jack, don't do that. You're drunk."

Callie was awestruck. "Unbelievable momma!" Maria returned to her story. She told Callie that Jack said, "Do you think that you are on vacation? She said, "I know I am not on vacation; but, if I wuz I wouldn't be round white people. I am going home." And she left.

After that story, Callie's Momma said, "Callie, I have always taught you to not spend your last and to always keep enough for a phone call." Maria went to a telephone booth and called her older brother, who had just bought a car, to come get her. Maria's brother informed Momma Maxine about the incident before his departure to get his sister. In the meantime, Miss Peters had called Momma Maxine to let her know that they would cut the trip short and bring Maria home.

Miss Peters called Maria back to the house. Everybody was there, including Jack. Miss Peters said, "I talked with Maxine. She agreed to let me bring you back home. We are cutting our trip short." Unexpectedly, Jack said, "Maria, I'm sorry. I was a little drunk." Maria responded, "Yes, you were."

Callie asked Maria this question: "Why did you have such uncontrollable anger when you were talking to Jack?" She answered, "I saw so many people done wrong by that family. Other white families in Monroeville treated people the same way."

When they brought Maria home, Momma Maxine felt ashamed and asked, "Why would you bring shame on our family?" Maria said, "I am not like you Momma." Momma Maxine's disposition was very gentle. Maria's siblings asked her, "Were you really going to hit him?" She reconfirmed, "I surely was going to hit him, if he hit me." They marveled at her boldness. They could not believe it. One of Maria's sisters who was old enough to be her Momma asked her, "How did it feel to talk to that man like that? Were you scared?" Maria answered, "No, I was not scared. He is just a man and that is all to it."

Momma Maxine said, "Maria, one day your mouth is going to get you into trouble." "It might get me into trouble, but it can also get me out of trouble." Still, Callie had another question that plagued her. She did not want to offend Maria; however, she needed to know the answer. "Momma" she inquired, "Are you prejudice? I want to know because of what you said about not wanting to go on vacation around white people." She said, "Yes, I am prejudice." Callie's heart dropped. "Momma, please help me to understand this. Did you say you were prejudice? Maybe, a better question is, were you prejudice against the evil things you saw or did you not like white people for their color?" Maria said, "I am prejudice. But then, it is because of how they treated Black people."

Maria's comment troubled Callie. So, if her Momma had said she hated white people for their color, that would have placed a tremendous strain on the mother-daughter relationship, since Callie knew how her great grandmomma treated granddaddy Louie.

As a child, Callie learned that her Momma spoke in strange ways. She had become accustomed to asking other questions to get the true meaning of what Maria was trying to convey. And this was one more example of why she needed to ask supplementary questions.

Essentially, Maria was a very righteous person. It didn't matter if a person were Black, white, red, or yellow, she would talk to you. The hatred she saw caused her prejudice and by coincidence it just so happened that most of the hatred she had seen or was exposed to, had been committed by white people.

Not much is known about Callie's Momma's family. What Maria learned about her family may have also added to her outlook. Maria told Callie that her great grandmomma was a slave on a plantation in Monroeville. She was from Africa, but she was freed a little time before she died. Her name was Little Sally Pope Jones. Maria's grandmomma was Bessie Pope and they called her Big Momma. She was a midwife and married Princeton Beauregard who worked at a sawmill. They had six children. The youngest was Momma Maxine.

What is interesting about prejudice in Monroeville is that it was not limited to Black people and Whites. It affected the African American race too. Light skinned

African Americans and dark-skinned African Americans had conflicts. No doubt, it carried over from the days of slavery. Moreover, there were different hues of color within the light-skinned African Americans. It was said, "The closer you are to white, you are always right." That statement created dissension.

Even if some light-skinned individuals did not feel that way, the saying was so deeply entrenched in the hearts and minds of some, it would prove futile to debate it. Based upon stories Callie read and heard, the lighter skinned African Americans were given better opportunities, better jobs. No wonder discord existed.

When Callie learned that her sister-in-law's family was a victim of prejudice, she asked her, "Why did yawl fight a good deal when you were growing up?" She said, "It was because my Momma was white, and she married my daddy who was Black. The kids called us names and made us feel bad about our parents." "You're joking, right? I always thought your Momma was just a light skinned Black person." Her sister-in-law giggled and asked, "You really thought my Momma was Black?" They both chuckled.

Many kids, including Callie, did not know how to interact with kids who were different from them or with different circumstances. Did heritage matter? That was debatable. And surely, many kids did not know how to handle money or understand the value of it, for Callie's momma would always ask her, "Do you think money grows on trees? She said, "Yes, money is made of paper and paper comes from trees." You can imagine what Maria said.

Callie learned that money did not grow on trees and most of the time, she had none growing in her bank account. She learned it was of utmost importance to educate children on how debt could bring about total devastation. When you consider the insatiable desire of the eyes that has the potential to lure anyone that can see into making unwise financial decisions, kids need ongoing training.

Chapter 3:   Childhood Basics

When adults asked Callie what she wanted to be when she grew up, she answered anything from a movie star to a lawyer. She loved watching reruns of the once popular television series, Gilligan's Island, which was about a movie star, professor, sailor, a married millionaire couple and others who were shipwrecked on a deserted island for many years. Next to that, she loved watching the television series Perry Mason, with the main character playing the role of a criminal lawyer who only lost one court case during the entire series. She loved dressing up, putting her momma's high-heeled shoes on, and pretending she was Ginger Grant, one of the main characters who played the movie star on Gilligan's Island.

Callie thought they had strong similarities, when the only similarity they shared was the mole they both had, centered on each one's face. Her momma thought she would make a good lawyer because she always asked so many piercing questions and she loved to talk.

Callie's earlier memories between four and five years old, however, were not of playing with the kids in the neighborhood or her siblings. She sought friendship with this large oak tree in the family's front yard that she named Mr. Botany. No one knew why Callie named the tree Mr. Botany, and for that matter no one knew if Callie could define botany. All that was known was she was very attached to the tree and like clockwork, every day after lunch, she would go outside to talk with Mr. Botany.

You would have thought Mr. Botany was one of the neighbors because everyone on their street knew him. Even the adults had respect for Mr. Botany, as did Mr. Curtis, one of the neighbors who stopped by to inquire about him, while Callie was having a conversation with Mr. Botany. Callie's response was, "If you don't get off Mr. Botany's roots, he will tell the ants to bite you." Mr. Curtis just laughed and went on his way.

Mr. Botany, however, presented a challenge for Callie's parents after a while because they wanted to start a construction project that would require them to destroy Mr. Botany. The construction would be a small juke joint as it was called in the south that would be a multi-faceted site with pool tables, a space for dancing and snacks to make money for the family.

They started clearing the land far from Mr. Botany's location. Yet as the days went by, the demolition crew got closer and closer to Mr. Botany. Callie went into a panic: "They are getting too close to Mr. Botany. Why are they doing that?" Her parents had not fully disclosed that Mr. Botany would have to be cut down. So, when they explained that to Callie, she started crying. She watched each day as the crew worked hard to remove the roots. Her parents watched her carefully to see if she would go into a temper tantrum as the bulldozer finished the job.

To their surprise she did not. Her emotions went the other way. Instead of going into a temper tantrum, she went into a deep depression without speaking one word about what had happened with Mr. Botany. It took about ten years after Mr. Botany's death when she was fifteen years old before Callie would bring closure to her ordeal. She wrote a letter to one of her good friends that knew Mr. Botany. In her letter, she expressed her grief and how she was trying to move forward. One excerpt from the letter read, "He was my best friend. He was there every day that I went outside, and he let me do most of the talking." Fortunately, the compassionate friend did not belittle Callie about a tree that had been long gone. That was perhaps, the single most crucial step Callie made to move forward with her deep loss- -to talk about how she felt. She had now made progress.

Although most of the neighbors on the street were Callie's relatives, the family across the street was very dear to her. Her cousin who was only two years older always watched out for Callie because she had severe health problems. Callie said to Maria in a very delicate voice: "Momma, the wind keeps blowing me down when I walk to the bus stop. It is so hard to stand up." Maria said, "Hold on to Bee while you are walking." Bee was nowhere near being frail. She was a very big girl who was quite nurturing for her age and treated Callie like she was her little living baby doll.

Now Maria had gotten sick to the point of not being able to care for Callie and the other children. Since Callie was the oldest and of school age, she had to go live with her grandmomma Maxine for a while because the school was near her house. Financially, it was hard for the family. The aid Callie would receive could only come from her grandmomma Maxine who Callie did not have a close relationship with ever.

During the time Callie lived with her grandmomma Maxine, she was in the first grade. Everything was so new for her. She was away from her cousin who had cared for her while walking to the bus stop. Her momma had fallen sick and let's not forget about Mr. Botany who had died. The fact that she knew no one else at school when the teacher assigned her to sit at the table with six-year-old boys, terrified her to the point of not making eye contact. Callie's momma Maxine nor the teacher knew that. This circumstance contributed even more to her health problems. The little boys would ask her to look under the table. They showed her things that she had never seen before. Each time they asked her to look under the table, she knew it was to show her something unsightly. However, she was afraid to say no.

Callie was afraid of everything. By the second grade, she was back home with her family. She didn't know what persuaded Maria to bring her back home with her other siblings, other than it was what she needed to happen. Those two little boys were criminals and eventually they dropped out of elementary school. Callie was happy not to ever see them again.

Callie's family outgrew their first house. Maria wanted a brand-new Jim Walter house and Callie's daddy, Raoul, agreed to build a house on land that he had bought from his sister. The cost of the house was a whopping fifteen thousand dollars. The house had three bedrooms, a den, two full bathrooms, a kitchen, dining room, living room and a laundry room. Maria was happy. Still, they had to be diligent about paying the house payment to keep it. They were successful, paying for the house in full within fifteen years. They budgeted wisely, so they could meet their goal.

The house did not have the glitz and glamour that many look for today when buying a house. Her parents were modest, and their modesty kept them from needlessly suffering anxiety because of financial worries, as well as it kept Callie from experiencing anxiety. She was very intuitive, and she could have easily absorbed her parents' anxiety.

Granddaddy Louie and others Callie knew were primarily cash customers back in the late sixties. At times, a lay-a-way plan was the only other possibility. Things changed for her granddaddy Louie in the early seventies. He showed her a credit card while she was visiting with him during spring break. Granddaddy Louie said, "Look heah, gurl. This is what cha call a credit card. You can buy anything you want wit dis lil card." Callie asked, "Where did you get that?" He said, "Your Uncle give it to me." He was fascinated with the card. Callie was cool. She did not say anything because she did not want to steal his thunder, as they say in the country. He had a can of raw oysters on the table, ready for a celebration. She celebrated with him; but she did not ever consider eating the raw slimy oysters to celebrate.

In the 1960's, when Martin Luther King Jr. had been very prominent in the fight for civil rights, Raoul told Callie many stories about what had occurred during that era. It meant very little to her. She simply did not understand or try to understand, since she felt it did not affect her. She did understand one thing.

When she was in the fourth grade in 1968, Martin Luther King Jr. had been shot to death and she saw how sad the people in their community were. Consistently, when others had emotional bouts, she absorbed their emotions. It was the same in this instance. Their sadness affected her enormously. There was no way she could fully appreciate his sacrifice. Since the emotional outburst of others sparked her interest, she wanted to learn more about him.

The tree that her parents had cut down and bulldozed had provided the space to build the little dance hall with a pool table and jukebox. Maybe, she could understand the sacrifice that Mr. King made. She walked over to the jukebox or record player to hear the speech Mr. King delivered in 1963 when she was five years old. Now she was nine years old, putting her money in the jukebox and pressing the buttons to hear his speech. She will never forget the crackling noise in the background on the record as Mr. King spoke.

To listen to his speech with the background noise did not bother her. She was focused on his words. She stayed there for the longest time replaying that speech. She memorized all the parts that said, "I have a dream" and especially the part that talked about the hope he had for his four little children. She was beginning to understand hope if nothing else.

Hope was an expectation of something good. Callie knew that could also apply to God who gives good things. The sentiments of his speech reminded her of a song that gives her hope to this day. The words are something like this:

Just see yourself, just see me too

Just see us all in a world that is new

Think how you'll feel, how it will be

To live in peace, to be truly free

No evil one will then prevail,

rule by our God cannot fail.

Mr. King's speech finally motivated this little nine-year-old girl sickly girl. And of course, she came to understand that we are all motivated by something. That we can never underestimate the impact our words can have on others. That words can either build us up or tear us down. More importantly, that words can either build others up or tear others down.

The school year had ended. Next year Callie would be in the fifth grade. Surprisingly, Maria gave her some exciting news. Momma Maxine was going to Boston, Massachusetts USA for the summer to visit relatives. So, Momma Maxine wanted Callie to go with her. Maria was happy because she was going to pay for all the expenses associated with the trip for the summer. The deep embarrassment Callie had experienced when she was unable to spell the four-letter word "debt," was now in the past. She was on her way to Boston for the summer.

As an adult looking back to her childhood, Callie could now see that she was such a deep thinker. While traveling with Momma Maxine by bus to Boston, yes, a bus for twenty-three hours, Callie was captivated by what she saw. As she studied the various shapes of the clouds, she wondered where God was in the whole scheme of things. Was it He who she was looking at in the clouds? She reasoned within herself that was virtually impossible, since God was so big. It did not come close to making sense. God had created the clouds. She continued meditating about the different shapes of the clouds as they traveled from city to city.

Around midnight or so, they were passing through Atlanta, Georgia when Callie saw this big, shiny, golden colored dome. She thought to herself, "This is where I am going to live when I grow up." She had never seen anything like that before. It was beautiful. Perhaps, this is the big city that her granddaddy Louie was talking about when she was younger.

They finally made it to Boston. Callie had done something none of her siblings or cousins in Clausell had ever done. She had traveled without her parents to a city that was over one thousand miles away. For the most part, the trip was a thrilling and educational adventure. She enjoyed getting to know her family; although, they talked strange to her. She experienced seeing an ice-cream truck drive through the neighborhood and she had never seen one before.

Callie had a unique talent. She could irrefutably explain anything that she had imagined, and she could believe that it was true. She used that talent on certain occasions. This is an occasion when Momma Maxine was upset with Callie. She did not at once respond to her call to come inside the house.

The children were playing a game of hide and seek near the house. Just as Callie found her place to hide, Momma Maxine called for Callie to come inside. Callie could not answer her just yet because if she did, she would give her location away. The kids would know where she was, and she would lose. She hated losing. Little did she know that it would send Momma Maxine into a hissy when she did not answer. Callie was thinking that the game would have been over in about five minutes. Then, she would let her grandmomma know why she did not answer her.

After the game was over, she told Momma Maxine what she did and her reasoning behind it. Momma Maxine told Callie that she was lying. Callie asked for the help of her cousins. How could you dispute this reasoning? Callie pointed to a location and said, "Momma Maxine, here is the exact location where you were standing when you called me to come into the house. You were near the middle of the porch, not far from the plant on the table. I had to be present to hear you and see you. You had your hand on one hip and the dish towel in the other hand. You did not have on any shoes. How would I know all of that if I had been down the street?" Momma Maxine said, "You are not telling me the truth. Do not lie to me. Where were you?" Callie dropped her head and went inside.

Although the explanation was very convincing and true, Callie did not take into consideration the fearfulness that Momma Maxine felt. She was too disturbed to accept her explanation. That one incident almost ruined the entire summer for Callie. She had a talent that was unique, but the timing of using it was off.

Moreover, Callie learned quite a bit from that episode. It was just a game with no prize. What would she have lost? She could have been kidnapped, especially with it being dusk dark outside. What if some devious person were hanging around for an opportunity to carry out a crime against her? Of course, she did not reason like that at nine-years-old. Looking back, the phrase referring to clearly seeing something and eventually understanding it is called,

"Hine sight is twenty-twenty." This convinced Callie to see and understand the potential danger that lurked when she did not answer Momma Maxine's call to come inside the house.

When Callie returned to Monroeville after her visit to Boston, Maria and Callie had a heart-to-heart conversation about her trip, particularly the one incident that almost ruined the trip for her and Momma Maxine. Callie shared what she thought was exceptional good news with Maria: "Momma, there was one thing that I really liked." Maria asked, "What was that Callie?" She had the biggest grin on her face when she said, "Momma, I am going to move to Atlanta when I get grown."

Maria had a slight smile and asked, "Callie, what do you know about Atlanta?" "Momma I know that I am going there when I get grown." She asked, "Why?" Callie replied, "I saw the city and it had a lot of lights. There was shiny gold all around the top half of one building. I liked it. It was so pretty." They never talked about Callie moving to Atlanta again until she was sixteen years old.

When you hear of a tragedy in a large city, you may empathize with the family even if you do not know the family personally. If you hear of a tragedy in a small town, it may be unbearable because it has possibly affected someone you know personally. If the tragedy involves a child, the feelings are compounded. That occurred in Clausell on Callie's street. As she was getting off the school bus, she was chatting with her neighborhood best friend. They were trying to decide if her friend's momma would bring the friend to Callie's house or if Callie's momma would let Callie go to her house. That day neither of them went to each other's house.

Within a couple of hours of their conversation, Callie's momma said, "Callie, I have some sad news. Barbara Ann died." She was shocked. She said, "Momma, I just talked to her. We were trying to decide whose house we would study at today. What happened?" Maria said, "She had complications with her sugar diabetes." Callie did not know what diabetes was. All she remembered was that they had eaten green apple stick candy on the bus. She thought that candy killed Barbara Ann because she was not supposed

51

to eat sugar. For years, Callie never ate green apple stick candy.

Maria did not allow Callie to go to the funeral. At the time, Callie did not know why she could not attend. Maria's decision was wise. Callie was in a daze, not being able to go to school for a few weeks. She missed Barbara Ann so much. It took almost twenty years before Callie stopped having dreams about looking for Barbara Ann in a closet, calling her name and upon awakening, she was soaking wet. The positive point was that Callie had no memories of her in a casket. Her last memory was of the two of them trying to make plans to study.

Other tragedies hit the small community in Clausell. Her cousin, Bee, who was her protector and one of eight children, lost her daddy in death. That was extremely difficult for the family because it was sudden. This was trying on many levels, especially financially. Conditions changed instantly. Bee's momma was a single parent with eight children under the age of seventeen years old. She had to take care of financial matters that her husband once handled, in addition to all her responsibilities she had prior to his death.

Death would not leave this family alone. Within a year, Bee's grandmomma died. Her grandmomma's heart ached after her son's death so very much that we could say, "She died of a broken heart." It's been said that it is just awful for a child to die before the parent. Callie saw how true that statement was concerning Bee's family. She learned that it does not matter how old or young the child is. Bee's daddy had a heart attack.

The heart attack was the result of a dislodged blood clot in his broken toe that traveled to his heart. Callie learned even more about death at an early age. Death created financial burdens for many in the community. Many families did not have life insurance, only burial policies. After the burial costs were covered, nothing was left for the family to continue with the daily necessities of life.

In that same family, Bee's granddaddy died about five years later. Callie was home from college. She was walking to her granddaddy Louie and Grandmomma Liz's house. On her way there, Callie waved at Bee's granddaddy as she passed. He was on the porch of one of the neighbor's house. She was not sure what he was doing. When she got up to her grandparents' house, she had just enough time to say hey to Grandmomma Liz when the telephone rang. Grandmomma Liz answered the phone. She hung the phone up and said, "Bee's granddaddy just died."

Callie said, "Grandmomma Liz, I just saw him at the neighbor's house. It cain't be. Grandmomma, I just saw him!" Grandmomma Liz said, "Come and give your grandmomma a hug. Your daddy said the roof on the porch fell on him and crushed him. Your daddy was the first one up there after he saw the roof falling. He tried to lift it off him but could not do it."

Callie cried, cried and cried. She made it back to her house that she grew up in as a teenager. It was one more tragedy. Many of the deaths that Callie had heard about took place without a person having an extended illness. Seeing and hearing about those tragedies that were so close to her made her think even deeper about life. When certain subjects came up, she was serious and had a no-nonsense attitude, especially when she heard people making comments about others playing hooky from work. Comments such as "He wasn't sick yesterday. She was laughing earlier. Now she's sick?" Callie often replied, "Maybe some people play hooky; but I have seen people that appeared to be fine and within the next few minutes, they were dead. I don't think it is fair to make assumptions. Sometimes we all make comments without thinking. We need to realize that there are many sensitivities in this world, and we should be empathetic to others because any one of us can get sick and die within a few minutes."

After Bee's granddaddy died, one of his daughters, who had attended the funeral earlier, was resting in the bed. She fell asleep while smoking a cigarette and the entire house burned down, killing her. The grief was overwhelming. Callie began to ask questions. "Why do we die? Why does God put us here to die?" Callie was confused and disturbed. She was not getting satisfying answers to her questions. But still, there were other puzzling things Callie would be introduced to during her life.

She was introduced to prejudice. This topic was coming up again. Her granddaddy had spoken about it. Her momma had spoken about it and now it was resurfacing. She did not understand why it was such a big issue to integrate the schools. She was happy attending the all-Black elementary school with all her friends. She was looking forward to going to the high school that her momma and daddy had attended.

She did not know much about the high school other than Maria's experiences she shared with her as she had never toured the inside of the high school. Her best memory of what high school would be like was at the parade that took place annually in the town square. There she saw the drum major with the long stick, as she called it, stepping high and the cheerleaders performing their stunts.

Yet, integration was occurring. The Black high school was closing. Callie had just graduated from the sixth grade and had anticipated going to high school in the fall. Elementary school consisted of grades one through six. High school was from the seventh to the twelfth grade. Obviously, she wanted to experience going to the high school that was closing.

Maria arranged for her to take a couple of classes in the summer before it closed in the fall. Her cousin-in-law taught one of the classes Callie attended. She was fascinated by what she was learning. He taught them about the different clouds, about the barometric pressure, about the stratosphere. Earlier, when she went to Boston for the summer, she was fascinated by the appearance of the different clouds as she and her grandmomma Maxine rode the bus. Now, she was learning about them. This class was incredible for Callie. She was experiencing high school and she was exhilarated.

Eventually, school integration occurred in Monroeville in the fall of 1971. The most embarrassing part about integration for Callie was the fact that she was returning to the school that she had just graduated from three months earlier. Her old school had integrated with grades starting from the first through the seventh. High school would now begin in the eighth grade instead of the seventh grade.

The first day of school was strange to her. It felt like she had regressed or failed somehow because she was going back to elementary school. She walked into homeroom and looked around to find a desk. She spotted a desk by this little white girl who was reading a book. This little girl never looked up to acknowledge Callie. Callie sat down and looked at her from head to toe. She could not believe her hair was so long. All of Granddaddy Louie's sisters had long wavy

57

hair. They were a mixture of French and Indian. One of her aunts had such long hair that when she wore it down, it almost touched her navel.

Callie was used to seeing hair longer than her hair. Of course, it was on older women. That's why she reasoned that it took all her aunt's life to get her hair that long. How did this little girl have hair that she could almost sit on? It was a mystery to her. Callie's hair was about four inches below her shoulder. She now wondered why her hair had not grown that long. Of all the things that she could have focused on, she focused on her hair.

Callie glanced around the room as the white kids entered. She was overcome for the kids spoke quite differently from her. They looked somewhat different than she. She even detected a slight difference in smell. They were very distracting; so, she went through a big adjustment period. At the end of the school year, she graduated again and moved on to the high school near town.

The fall was here. Callie was officially in high school. The year was 1972. The campus was much different from what she had seen at the high school that she attended in her community during the previous summer. For one thing, there were more children. Integration had done a number on her self-esteem. Callie couldn't see where she fit in and she felt that the white kids were smarter, more advanced and she could not handle it. Callie needed a coach, a tutor, someone, anyone to prepare her for a culture that was foreign to her.

During homecoming, the recent integration still had many nervous. The high school board decided to have a black queen and a white queen for each grade. It made things a little easier. It seemed like the right thing to do to reduce possible race problems.

Callie did not know how she got on the ballot; but she was elected as the black homecoming queen for the eighth grade, and she was surprised she won. With her vivid imagination, she came up with a likely reason why she got the title. Her cousin was a senior who was very popular. She was on the ballot, and she won the seat of homecoming queen. Many of the kids thought that Callie was her little sister. The kids would ask, "Are you Jordan's little sister?" She would respond, "No, she is my cousin." Since Jordan and Callie shared the same last name and they were both on the ballot, Callie imagined that she got the votes from the seniors who voted for her cousin. She did not mind the attention.

It was a great introduction to high school for her and Callie certainly did not object to being in her cousin's shadow. In this instance, integration seemed okay. Experiences like this may have contributed to Callie's thinking that everything will work out. What she would later learn was that not all challenges work out for the good.

Chapter 4: Financial Lessons Learned

Callie inherited her entrepreneurial spirit from her daddy's side of the family. She bought a type of Popsicle named Kool Pops from the local store owned and operated by a family member. A Kool Pop was in a container about the size of a twelve-inch ruler. Once you opened the top of the Kool Pop, you could squeeze the bottom to push the frozen treat out. It seemed like it was not a complicated recipe and a clever idea for Callie to make them and sell them herself.

Kool-Aid was the drink to consume when Callie was a child because it was economical and something all family members could enjoy. It came in a variety of flavors for only ten cents per package. All you had to do was pour the contents of one package, about the size of the palm of your hand, into a large pitcher, add water and sugar to taste. Callie invested in one package of Kool-Aid which made a full pitcher, borrowed the sugar and water from Maria's kitchen, poured it into several ice trays and sold the frozen Kool-Aid cubes to her relatives.

The cost was five cents for two cubes with twenty cubes in each tray. Yes, they sold and at a profit! Callie did that until she had a conflict with one of her cousins. Would you believe that he no longer wanted to pay five cents for the two frozen cubes, which he had bought regularly? Callie had stipulated from the beginning that the customer had to buy two cubes. He wanted to buy only one cube at two cents. The obvious conclusion is that he wanted something that he could not afford, and he did not have enough money. He was addicted to the treat and because of his addiction, he was aggressive toward Callie. Though frightened by his aggression, Callie did not back down on her price, two cubes for five cents.

She did not do well handling that conflict. She stopped making the frozen treats for she did not want to fight with her male cousin. While not wanting to encounter conflict, little did Callie know that it was not healthy to always quit something to avoid conflict. Callie learned later that if she continued to quit just to avoid a conflict, she would be labeled a quitter. Besides that, Callie would learn that some people may try to sabotage your hard work. This may be in the form of backing out on agreements previously made.

Somehow along the way, Callie learned the value of contributing financially to her family. At fifteen years old, Callie asked Maria to help her get a job with one of her cousins who owned a flower shop. Callie worked there for about three years. Her cousin taught her how to make all kinds of floral designs. She made bridal bouquets, funeral wreaths, arrangements for the altar at the church and floral arrangements for her home. Since it was the only flower shop in Clausell, Callie had gotten pretty good at designing floral arrangements because business was good. The family was very proud of her, especially Granddaddy Louie.

While sitting on the couch with his legs curled to his side, hardly ever using her name, Granddaddy Louie asked Callie, "Hey Gurl, do you want a flower shop? If you want one, I'll buy it for ya." Where did that come from? Maybe, he asked because he was a businessman. Maybe, he asked since there was only one flower shop and his cousin owned it. Maybe, he wanted to give his family member competition. Maybe when he looked at the two large floral arrangements in front of the church's altar on Sunday mornings, he remembered that Callie had made them.

Callie didn't know why he offered to buy her one. There was no need to deliberate about the reason because Callie had a made-up mind and she replied, "No-o-o Granddaddy, I have other plans." He laughed so hard until his stomach jumped up and down. Then Callie started laughing. Granddaddy Louie never brought that subject up again.

When Callie began working at the flower shop, her hours worked were Monday through Friday, from three p.m. to five p.m. On Saturday, she worked nine a.m. to five p.m. She earned thirty-five dollars per week. Sometimes, Callie had to work in the evenings around seven p.m. for an hour or so if there were a wake at the funeral home.

Callie made a few extra dollars opening the flower shop during that time. You see, her family member who owned the flower shop also owned the funeral home and the insurance agency. If there were a wake or viewing of the body, Callie had to open the flower shop in the evening just in case someone wanted to buy flowers.

This was the normal routine when a wake was scheduled. Callie closed the shop promptly at five p.m. She walked home, got something to eat, changed her clothes and came back to re-open the shop. The funeral home was on a big hill across the street from the flower shop. As soon as someone ordered flowers for the deceased, Callie had to deliver them to the funeral home and place them in the booth where the body was found for viewing. Callie had previously informed her cousin that if a corsage or boutonnière were ordered for the deceased, Callie would deliver it. Except, she would not pin it on the body.

During this week, Callie was running back and forth from the flower shop to the funeral home to deliver flowers. Since there was not a funeral home in the nearby county, many of the Black people had their funerals conducted in Clausell. Because of the number of wakes that week, she was very busy. Right before she was about to close the flower shop, Callie received an order for a boutonnière for a man that was about sixty-five years old.

She made it, took it up to the funeral home and dropped it in the casket near his chest and ran back down to the shop. On her way down the hill, her cousin and the funeral home attendant were leaving so they could come back early for the wake. Callie told them she was leaving too as soon as she got back down the hill.

When Callie got down to the flower shop, she gathered all her things and headed out the door. As she was locking the door, the telephone rang. Callie came back to answer it. It was an order for a floral arrangement. Callie explained to the customer that she was the only one on the premises. She explained graciously that she could only prepare a potted plant before the wake because she did not have enough time to make anything more. The customer accepted that, and Callie assured him that it would be there before the wake started.

Callie dressed the potted plant with a nice blue paper around the bottom and made a huge blue bow. After she had given her word that it would be there before the wake started, Callie felt that she should deliver it before she left for home just in case, she was running a little late getting back. Again, Callie ran up the hill. The deceased must have been very popular because she had made so many floral arrangements. Remembering earlier that she had dropped the boutonnière in the casket, Callie checked to see if the funeral home attendant had pinned it on the deceased before he left. He had. However, Callie noticed something else or perhaps didn't notice something else on her prior visits.

The deceased had glasses on his face. All during her time of running back and forth, Callie never noticed that. She thought to herself, "Hmm. That's strange." As she was re-arranging the other flowers to find a spot for the baby blue potted plant, the lights went out. Callie threw that pot down and started running. No one was supposed to be on the premises but her. How were those lights turned out? It did not matter. Callie was gone.

It was as if a match had been struck and was meeting combustible fluids and she was trying to get away from it. A few steps more she would have been out of the door. Then, Callie ran into a person that grabbed her and she started hitting the person in the chest, trying to make her way to the door. He screamed, "Callie, it's me." She recognized the voice, and it was the funeral home attendant. He wasted no more time turning the light switch on to calm Callie. He was doubled over with laughter and could not stop. On the other hand, Callie was livid and yelled, "You have to clean up everything and straighten it out. I am going home!"

Callie cannot tell you what motivated her to stay in a job that kept her on edge. She can only come up with the answer that she just wanted the job very much. Besides that, there were few other options for work in Monroeville. Maria recalled Callie always telling her about the dead people she saw at the funeral home. She wondered how Callie could manage. She asked, "Callie, does that bother you? How can you sleep at night?" Callie replied, "Yes, I am scared. I try not to think about it. I just look at it like that's part of the job to just drop the order off and keep going."

When Callie turned sixteen and got her driver's license, she was given another responsibility at work. She handled picking up the floral arrangements for the church she attended plus placing them at the altar before the 11:00 a.m. service began. She received more responsibility without any increase in pay. Yet, it did not matter to her because of the opportunity to learn.

Her favorite arrangement was made with yellow gladiolas as well as yellow chrysanthemums. Callie started the arrangement by placing greenery at the back of the container. Next Callie took five gladiolas and placed them in front of the greenery. One of the gladiolas was at the center of the arrangement, the focal point, along with two gladiolas on each side of the one in the middle, giving the appearance of a wide "V."

Callie placed chrysanthemums, baby's breath and other fillers to make the arrangement appear fuller. The two arrangements were quite large. Previously, they were delivered by van before her cousin asked her to transport them to the church. Callie wrestled with them, struggling to fit them into the back seat of her car. Although she worked at the flower shop for three years, she performed that task alone for two years.

At times, Callie was distracted in church when she noticed that a flower may not have been centered or she did not fully carry out the look that she had designed and wanted to see. Those times were few. Yet, if that were the case, Callie felt like asking the preacher, "Would you please stop talking? Let me fix this arrangement. It is driving me out of my mind. I am not listening to you. I cannot focus."

Callie's responsibilities were varied and kept increasing. This next task was a fun project. Her employer cousin asked her to babysit her grandchildren while they visited for the summer. Her cousin asked, "Callie would you take my grandchildren to the movies?" Callie didn't have a problem with that request. She said, "Yes, I would love to do that." The cousin asked, "Could you also drive them there please?" "No problem. I can do that too." Of course, Callie would get paid. Her payment would be a ticket to the movies with popcorn and drink. Callie received instructions, though, that made her skeptical about going to the movies. Her cousin said, "I don't want my grandchildren going upstairs to the balcony to sit. Please purchase tickets for the main auditorium."

"What?" Callie thought. She was afraid to voice her concerns out loud. She contemplated how she was going to do that because she had never sat in the main auditorium. Callie had only seen whites sit in the main auditorium. Her cousin, Ester, looked white, so she never had a problem. Callie, on the other hand, had a tan making her look like a person of Mediterranean descent. So, she had much more of an ethnic color tone. Black people always sat in the balcony. That's where Callie and all her sisters used to sit. The cousin gave Callie money for their tickets, popcorn and drinks. The cost to sit in the balcony was fifty cents. The cost to sit in the main auditorium was two dollars.

Callie was not sure how the attendant would respond to her request to buy tickets for the main auditorium. It was 1974. The school system had just integrated in 1971. Callie had never seen Black people work there either. Given that, you see how troubling that could be for her. As soon as she pondered how she would be treated for requesting a ticket to the main auditorium, something eased her mind. It was a matinee to see a cartoon feature. Perhaps, many people would not attend. Callie asked the young woman in the ticket booth, "I would like to purchase three tickets for the floor in the main auditorium." Hardly anyone was there, more specifically, just the three of them sat in the auditorium. Each of them had their choice of sitting wherever they liked. Callie chose to sit close, about three rows from the screen and the grandchildren joined her.

What an experience for her since she had never been that close to a movie screen in her entire life. The screen was massive, and the details were captivating. After the movie was over, Callie took the children home. When she informed Maria where they sat, Maria said, "I have never sat down there either." Callie's prayer was answered.

Callie received other assignments that were not related to floral designing when work was slow at the flower shop. Several times, her cousin asked her to perform household chores or roller set her hair. The payment for Callie was a private swim in her cousin's big pool with beautiful blue water. Surely, Callie loved relaxing in the water; nevertheless, she did not want to do any of those other tasks. Somehow, she felt that it was not right, and she was being taken for granted. She complained to her momma asking, "Momma, why do I have to roller set her hair, or fold clothes, or dust and all those other household chores?" Maria was upset; but, tried to be encouraging saying, "Baby, it's not right, but go ahead and learn what you can." Callie just wanted to make the floral arrangements. At any rate, Callie did those other tasks to the best of her ability.

A benefit of doing what Callie did not want to do early in life, prepared her for working outside of her primary job description, an ability that was greatly used later in life. For example, when a person is hired to do a specific job, a list of the primary responsibilities of the job is outlined. Here is the catch.

The final statement in the job description is almost always stated, "Performs other duties as assigned." Callie learned from working at the flower shop how to be adaptable. She learned how to be submissive. She learned how to be a team player. She learned how to take the initiative.

There was one thing that kept Callie focused, the check. Callie would cash her check at the bank, place a small amount in her savings account and disperse the rest. This is how the disbursement went. She put five or ten dollars in her savings account. This was based upon what she earned for the week. More often, Callie made thirty-five dollars to forty dollars for the week.

Callie gave Raoul ten dollars, Maria five dollars, and one dollar to each of her siblings. She kept the rest, which was not very much. No one told her to do that, she just wanted to do it. It seemed like the responsible thing to do from her perspective. Maria did not want to take the money. She said, "Just give some to your daddy, not me." Callie convinced her otherwise. Callie saved her money for big purchases, like when she bought her car and her class ring.

Callie was a busy young person. She played the piano for Sunday school and Vacation Bible School. Callie did not get paid by the church for that service. One of the little old ladies in the church must have known that and would consistently give Callie five dollars per week after she played the piano. She always found Callie and pressed it into her hand after the service.

Maria did an excellent job in showing her children how she paid the bills. Callie's parents had no significant debt, the typical mortgage and car payment or "car note," as they said in the country. They had no credit cards. Maria saved a little money. Callie cannot speak about what Raoul saved because he did not tell her. Maria had a Christmas Fund and a vacation fund. Her company deducted a specific amount of money from her paycheck for each of these funds. In addition to that, she kept a regular savings account at the local bank.

Callie's husband, Pierre and his family were similar in a few ways to Callie's family. His grandmomma was a powerful help while he was younger and was very active in his life. His momma spent a lot of time telling him how to prepare for success. When he worked, she asked that he save all his money. This would allow Pierre to get ahead and have the needed funds when making his purchases. She taught him how to cook several dishes because she knew that Pierre could save money by cooking at home. Pierre's daddy was a lot like Callie's daddy. They did not communicate about financial matters.

Pierre's grandmomma raised him along with his two brothers. When Pierre lived with his grandmomma, he learned to pay for things. She was no nonsense. And she knew the boys needed discipline if they were going to be responsible men. She prepared them to take care of a wife and children. Pierre's momma needed the strength of her momma to provide a stable environment for the boys. Small town living would do just that. They always lived in a house and his momma helped his grandmomma financially to fulfill that enormous responsibility.

Raoul bought his family's first home from Granddaddy Louie at a tiny price of twenty-five hundred dollars. It was a little three-bedroom house on about five acres of land. The two main streets in the community were named after Raoul's family. The names were Clausell Road and Clausell Quarters. Eventually, Raoul decided to clear some of the land and build a little juke joint, as they were called in the South.

On one side of the shop, land was cleared where the children could play softball. Raoul's talents were many. In addition to his job as a foreman, he was a mechanic, a barber, a carpenter and the owner of a pool hall. This allowed the family to have extra income from time to time.

Raoul was a hard worker to a degree. His vices undermined his ability to progress. His vices were gambling, alcohol and women. Those vices certainly affected the family financially. Callie did not know how much it affected the family. Still, she knew that it smothered his potential for financial growth. Maria worked outside of the home although Raoul did not want her to work. Callie always felt their family would do better financially if they moved to a larger city.

Raoul felt the same about moving to a larger city, while Maria did not want to leave her friends and family. Time would tell if Callie's hunch was correct or incorrect. Callie could judge the results or outcome of the situation, and the verdict was that staying in Monroeville did Raoul no good.

Maria and Raoul always had arguments. It could be about any or all his vices. Callie was the oldest of the children. She would ask Maria not to say anything that would start an argument, as Callie would say, "Momma, I want to sleep tonight." Because Maria was such a highly spirited person and she would not let Raoul get away with anything, it would cause arguments. In many cases, Raoul was wrong, but it was Maria's sarcastic comments that triggered these arguments.

The arguments affected all the children and many of the relatives. Despite all the good things Callie learned from Maria and Raoul, Callie was tired of viewing their life of bitter dissension. Callie was exhausted from the sleepless nights, the arguments, and whatever else disturbed the family's peace.

She did her best to cope. One way was by making a joke about their conflicts. Naturally, that did not always work. One time while talking to Maria, Callie whispered, "Momma, in two more years I will be on my way to Atlanta." Callie made the comment in a matter-of-fact way, and she did not care whether Maria heard it or not because it primarily served as a reminder for Callie to stay focused.

Initially, when Callie spoke to Maria about her plans to move to Atlanta, Callie was nine or ten years old. It was a delightful feeling. Now, her feeling had changed. The happiness she once enjoyed had shifted to unhappiness. Her only choice was to stay focused on not giving up. Callie noticed a pattern. Anytime she had some type of opposition or challenge, it would affect her. Callie realized she had not been coached on how to handle adversity or challenges in a positive way. Watching how others responded to adversity was how she, at times, handled problems. That was not an effective way to learn. Callie had to find another way to cope with her parents' discord. She got involved in extracurricular activities at school.

Could it be that Callie had taken on granddaddy Louie's demeanor? He did not want "anythang live." He did not say how long he felt that way. Well, Callie did not want to deal with her "live" parents' problems. Maria felt that Callie did not care about the family. But to Callie, it was the best way that she could survive emotionally.

Chapter 5: The Teenage Years

Callie had a crush on Roger, the neighborhood boy. It was clear that Maria did not like him and at times, Raoul felt the same. Then there were times when Raoul treated Roger like he was his best friend. That was very frustrating for Callie.

Around 10:00 p.m. everyone was at home asleep, except Raoul. Raoul coasted into the yard, blew the horn and called out to Callie: "Callie, Roger was in a car accident." Callie was a light sleeper, so she went to the door to see what was going on. Raoul repeated what he said earlier, "Roger was in a car accident. Come on. I'll take you to see him." They could hear him because the bedroom Callie shared with her sisters was at the front of the house.

Well, Callie grabbed her bathrobe to put over her gown and ran out of the house to go with her Daddy. The police station was about two miles away, so it took only minutes to get there. When they walked in, Roger was sitting in the lobby. He smiled and asked, "What are you doing here?" Callie said, "Daddy brought me here. He told me you had a car accident. Are you ok?" Roger explained that his red Mustang was totaled but he did not sustain any serious injuries. He looked dazed and very tired. His classic red mustang was gone forever. After that brief dialogue, Raoul brought Callie back home.

Callie's momma was awake and waiting. Raoul dropped Callie off at home and said, "I'll see you later." As soon as Callie walked in, Maria started fussing at her. She said, "Why did you leave without telling me? Callie explained, "When Daddy tells you to do something, you don't hesitate. You move quickly." Callie was confused as to why Maria was angry with her, when it was her other parent who had taken her. Callie would not have known anything if he had not gotten her out of bed. That was a battle that Callie was not going to win. His accident occurred about a week before her sixteenth birthday.

Her parents had planned to give her a sweet sixteen birthday party. Callie invited fifty people from Monroeville. On the day of her party, the weather was beautiful with no rain in sight. The refreshments were prepared, and the music was thumping. Her guests started to arrive while cars parked all along the roadside, bumper to bumper.

The building was swarming with teenagers who were invited and with teenagers who were not invited, of which that did not matter much to Callie because she was turning sixteen years old. Given that, Maria went into a fit of anger, transforming into a Grinch. She shouted, "Where are all these people coming from?" Callie said, "I don't know. Momma, please it is really good!" Callie was extremely excited and happy. Although she did not know the teenagers who were not invited, she reasoned they must have been from the neighboring town. She also knew how difficult it was to find entertainment and for that reason, she was happy that they thought about coming to celebrate with her.

Then the embarrassment began. Maria started running teenagers away in conjunction with taking food out of some of the guests' hands. Maria said, "They are just coming in and grabbing plates of food and leaving." Maria was tight on the dollar. Giving her the benefit of the doubt, Maria was just looking at the potential cost of all the food and the possibility of it running out.

Seeing that Maria already did not like Roger, she was upset that he had not come to her daughter's party. Maria kept asking Callie, "Where is Roger? Where is he Callie?" Callie had so much going on with all her guests that she hardly noticed he had not come. Maria was angry with the invited teenagers that came, and she was angry with the uninvited teenagers that came. The emotional cost to Callie was just as bad as the financial cost to Maria. Callie resolved then not to ever have another birthday party or any party again while living at home. And Callie stayed true to her resolve.

Raoul, trying to patch things up after the party said, "Callie I know you wanted a car when you turned sixteen. I found one for you in Mobile. The owner is a little old lady that has kept it in good condition. If you want it, I will get it for you. You would have to pay for it though." Callie asked, "How much is it?" He said, "Two hundred dollars." "Oh daddy, yes I want it. When can I get it?" "I will get it this weekend." Callie went to the bank to get the two hundred dollars from her savings and gave it to her daddy to pay for the car.

Raoul brought the car home for Callie. All in the family came out to inspect it. It was canary yellow with white leather seats. The condition of the car was immaculate, big enough to carry six people with no scratches or dents. And what is more, Callie loved yellow. She nicknamed it "the bat mobile" because of the long-pointed tail on the car.

Since her daddy was a mechanic, Callie had no worries about car maintenance. Maria had agreed to pay for the insurance. Her only challenge was filling the tank with gas. Raoul agreed to give Callie a tank of gas per week, since Callie bought the car. Callie did not mind sharing her car because she loved to walk. She walked to work and other places that was within a mile or so of her house. She would ride her bike if it were longer distances within Monroeville. She would just want to use the car primarily for long distance trips to visit her friends in the next town.

The arrangement Raoul had made with Callie about supplying her with a tank of gas per week worked for a while until Callie did something to make her daddy angry. Callie had left home early Saturday morning to go to her friend's house in Finchburg, about eighteen miles away. Even though Maria asked how long Callie would be gone, Callie gave a vague answer: "I will be gone all day."

Callie did exactly what she said she was going to do. She went to Finchburg early in the morning and was gone all day. She and her friend left Finchburg and went to Mobile, a little over an hour's drive away. When Callie got home, Maria asked her where she had gone. Callie answered, "I went to Finchburg." Callie felt that was not a lie neither did she want to tell her everywhere else she had gone.

Her dad, being the detective along with investigator reporter, told Maria that Callie must have gone somewhere else. He said to Maria, "Callie had about two hundred additional miles on her car." "What? What do you mean?" Callie asked. He then told Callie, "I checked the mileage before you left. I checked it again when you got back home." The good news was that he did not take the car from Callie at that time. He just stopped giving Callie a tank of gas per week.

Being the innovative type, Callie came up with an idea. The Bat Mobile could comfortably fit six people. Gas was thirty-nine cents per gallon; so, anyone that rode in her car had to give her fifty cents per ride. That worked well. Callie even made a small profit, *Cha-ching.*

Callie's favorite subjects were English and Creative Writing. She loved to talk and loved to ask questions, a great combination for a career in the legal field. Mr. MacArthur, her high school English teacher, thought highly of her writing skills. He often read her essays to the class. Sometimes, Callie was happy about it. Other times, it embarrassed her.

She was getting closer to her high school graduation, the last step before her move to Atlanta. A few days prior to her high school graduation, Raoul knocked on her bedroom door; so, Callie invited him in to have a seat. He congratulated Callie for her upcoming graduation from high school. None of her sisters were in the room. As he glanced around the room, he noticed the white French Provincial dresser and beds, the frilly pillows and bed covering that complimented a girl's room. Then his eyes moved toward the end of her bed, and he inquired about the trunk. Callie answered, "It's for my clothes that I am taking to Atlanta." He was surprised: "For your clothes you are taking to Atlanta? Does your momma know that?" Callie said, "Yes daddy." Raoul asked another question. "How long has she known that?" "I told momma when I was nine or ten years old and reminded her again when I was almost sixteen." "Well, she did not tell me." Raoul admitted.

When Callie told him that, he left her room to find Maria in the kitchen. He exploded: "Maria, is it true that Callie told you she was moving to Atlanta?" Maria responded, "Yeah Raoul. She told me that. During that time, I did not pay any attention to what Callie said. She was just a little girl." Then Callie said, "Momma, I told you again when I was almost sixteen." "Yeah, I know. But you didn't mean that." "Yes, I did." Her daddy, who appeared happy and proud of Callie's accomplishment ten minutes ago now appeared dangerous. Raoul educated Callie on her decision with this comment: "If you leave to go to Atlanta Callie, I will disown you. You are not going to have everybody wondering why you left home so soon." What a mistake Raoul was about to make with his oldest daughter.

Maria asked Callie not to leave right after graduation for the simple reason that Raoul would really disown her. While reasoning with Callie, Maria lamented, Callie, your daddy has let his pride get in the way and he will not lose face. If you leave, he will disown you." Callie's frustration caused a sarcastic response, "Momma, that's not a bad idea. That would be a blessing for me." Maria started crying. If Maria did not take Callie seriously earlier, she knew now that Callie was serious. "Callie, why did you wait until now to discuss this?" "Momma, I did not wait. You just did not take me seriously. What good would it have been to keep talking about it, when I recognized you did not believe me the first time."

With a gloomy face, Maria slowly swallowed: "Callie, if you need anything, your daddy would be the one to help you." The conversation was getting tense when Callie blurted out an awfully disrespectful response: "He has never done anything for me. It was always you. He was too busy doing other things and now he wants to pretend like I am at fault. I don't care anymore." Now Callie was angry! Maria made this request, "Then just do it for me. Stay a little longer. Please don't leave right away." Seeing her momma break down, Callie acquiesced, "Okay Momma, I will do it for you." Callie postponed her departure for two weeks.

Considering that Callie was a very soft spoken and obedient child this was surely upsetting to her that the discussion escalated to a point that caused so much pain for all the participants in the conversation. She was in the middle of the worse conflict that she had met thus far in her life. Still, she knew that a few tears could not change her mind forever. She would just give her parents enough time to digest the seriousness of her move to Atlanta.

Callie thought she was being gracious in postponing her trip for two weeks. Raoul would not let it rest. He did not want it to appear that Callie was leaving to get away from home. What else did he imagine. He knew that was the reason. He knew what life was like in their household and that Callie was different. She had mildly warned them on many occasions that she did not like the arguing. What would they expect her do? Raoul, Maria and all the children were quietly holding on to the belief that they were a "perfect" family. Truth be told, there are no perfect families. Arguing every week was just as out of the norm as eating dirt. For all the good things that Callie learned from her parents, one negative aspect, constant conflict diluted much of their hard work.

Callie would often say to her momma, "All of us should have gone to Hollywood for our acting abilities. Daddy should have won an Academy Award! Momma, you should have won Best Supporting Actress!" Maria would just laugh and say, "Callie, you are so funny."

Callie's leaving may have revealed to close family members that she was running away; but others did not have a clue. In fact, going to Atlanta started out as a goal when Callie saw the capitol of Atlanta on her way to Boston for the summer. It was a happy time. She felt she was in harmony with what Granddaddy Louie told her about getting out of Monroeville. Then things changed in her family, and it grew into being a necessary urgent departure. Callie wanted to experience peace and happiness, so she could not stay in Monroeville any longer.

Raoul said, "Ok, if you leave, you leave without your car." Callie did not respond because she did not like how the other explosion had occurred. She felt bad about her interaction with her parents on that occasion. Thus, Callie was moving forward with her plan without a vehicle. She called her Uncle Javier, who lived in Atlanta, and asked him to pick her up.

When her Uncle turned up two weeks later in Monroeville to bring Callie to Atlanta, all the family gathered outside to wave goodbye to Callie, except her daddy. Callie was so happy, as were her siblings, but Maria cried like a baby. The big city, Atlanta, was where Callie dreamed of being. She knew she belonged there just as her granddaddy Louie knew that she belonged there too.

Life began to change for her when she enrolled in a community college in Atlanta. She was so happy to live with her Uncle Javier for about five months. During the summer, Callie had agreed to pay her way by babysitting his three small children. Again, her feelings of making a monetary contribution surfaced.

Although Callie was bartering with her Uncle, she wanted to do more. She went grocery shopping with money that she had saved, spending over one hundred dollars in food for the family. She bought things that the children would especially enjoy. Uncle Javier was impressed with her purchase. He commented, "You didn't have to do that." Callie called out to him, "I wanted to. I feel better when I can contribute, whether small or large."

Her uncle bought a brand-spanking-new Ford car, never driven off the car lot by another person. The exterior color of the car was forest green with a tan interior, and he was very particular about that car. Because Callie had shown him, she was responsible, her Uncle allowed her to use the car for an entire day. Callie's friend came to visit her, and Callie asked if she would like to drive the car around the block. Javier's six-year-old daughter told her daddy, "Someone else drove your car daddy. It was a lady with very short hair."

Javier asked Callie, "Did somebody else drive my car?" Callie said, "My friend drove it. But I was in the car with her. I just let her drive it around the block. I promise that was the only distance that she drove." Javier scolded her saying, "You should be very happy that nothing happened to my car. How could you do that? You better not do that again." Callie learned that when someone loans you their prized possession, take care of it. And she also learned she should not have been so generous with something that did not belong to her.

Uncle Javier always thought large. He had a fantastic job working with Ford Motor Company. Anyhow, that was not good enough for him. He spoke regularly about becoming a millionaire. He was the only person that Callie could remember who had dreams of that size. Although he had a respectable job, being confined to hourly wages and set hours was just not him.

When he spoke about becoming rich, he was one half step away from giving the appearance that he was going into a convulsion. For instance, one day he said to Callie, "I got this deal Callie. If I can get one thousand people to buy into it, I will be well on my way to becoming a millionaire." While speaking, the pitch of his voice got higher and higher. He would not let her get one word in as he would raise his voice to keep control. Then he started breathing hard to keep going at the pace of his conversation.

He lived for becoming financially independent like Callie lived for moving to Atlanta. His friends would only stare at him in amazement. His zeal for becoming wealthy was over the top, so much so that when he talked about it, his smile appeared to show at least twenty of his teeth. Callie was hyper-sensitive to his zeal. She thought that if he did not stop speaking about becoming wealthy, he would do anything to achieve it. She was correct in her assessment, and she was his first target.

Repeatedly, he would try to seduce her and other listening ears into buying into his thinking about quick get rich schemes that were totally unreasonable, if not, unethical to Callie. He eventually left quit his job at Ford and pursued a career in real estate. This seemed more realistic in carrying out his first goal of not being confined to hourly wages and set working hours. In any case, there was a lot to be done before becoming a big shot millionaire.

Something ensued that reconfirmed to Callie she needed a car. Uncle Javier lived in an area that was about one-half mile from the bus stop. Callie was almost home when a suspicious looking car passed by her, stopping about ten to fifteen feet ahead of her. The driver pulled over to the side of the road, got out of the car and started walking toward Callie. She knew it was a male, but she could not see his facial features clearly. He said, "Hey, do you need a ride?" As he approached, Callie moved to the center of the road from the sideline and yelled, "No, I am okay. I live right around the corner!" He got back into his car and drove off. When he left, Callie did not stop running until she made it home.

She called Maria to tell her what had happened. Maria said, "Your daddy is not going to let you bring your car to Atlanta." Somewhere in the conversation, Maria decided to let Callie use her car. She brought the car to Callie. Within a month of using Maria's car, Raoul instructed Maria to have Callie bring the car back to Monroeville; so, she complied with his request to bring the car home. She drove the car to Monroeville, left it with Maria and returned to Atlanta the same day by bus.

Still, she needed transportation. Callie knew that her daddy would not change his mind about her bringing the Bat Mobile to Atlanta even after he knew how dangerous it was for her to walk from the bus stop. Callie knew the real reason that Raoul was so hard was that he just wanted her to come back to Monroeville to live. On top of that, he was not even speaking to Callie.

Uncle Javier decided to let Callie buy his old car. He said that he could not stand it if something bad happened to her because she did not have transportation. Uncle Javier, who had helped Callie in getting to Atlanta, sold Callie his old car for three hundred dollars. He would have given it to Callie; except, Callie had this thing about paying her own way. Also, Uncle Javier was concerned that the car was not reliable for long trips. Callie assured him that it would be okay.

It was beige with a black interior. It served the purpose that Callie needed to get back and forth to college and work. She was never concerned about year, make or model of the car. Neither was she concerned about going to a car wash to have it cleaned. That would have cost money that Callie wanted to use for other things; so, she washed the car herself.

Callie had finished washing her car when she threw the bucket of unclean water into the grass. Off came two of her most expensive pieces of jewelry. It was a ring with an emerald setting that her daddy gave her when she turned sixteen and her class ring which she bought with the money she had saved. Her class ring was smaller and very feminine, and it cost more money than the regular class rings. Now, within one year, Callie had thrown it away in the grass. She tried to find it that night but could not. The next day Callie tried again and was unsuccessful. She knew that being overly attached to a material item would not be healthy for her; so, Callie moved on and counted it as a loss.

Callie continued to babysit for her Uncle Javier while in her first quarter in college. During the winter break, she found a job opening in a flower shop in downtown Atlanta. The owner and Callie talked about her experience, and he hired her that day. Callie assumed she knew a lot about flowers when she started working there. She saw flowers that she had not heard of before. She was the youngest of the floral designers. Besides that, she was confident about her abilities until she saw the work that two of the designers produced. One of them could have been her grandmomma. She treated Callie like she was her granddaughter and assisted Callie with many of the complicated designs.

At the flower shop where Callie worked in Clausell, she had latitude to design whatever floral arrangement she wanted to make or simply make what Callie thought was pretty. At this shop, the customers would select an arrangement from a book and then the designer would make it.

She learned what teamwork was all about. This business ran like an assembly line in a factory. When the designers had completed their workload, they would help her complete her work or teach her new things. Callie was so thankful and wanted to repay them. Then she noticed that the two designers who helped her did not own a car; so, she volunteered to take them home after work. They accepted the time-consuming gift from her, which proved extremely generous after a hard day's work.

The woman who could have been her grandmomma had a husband whose illness prevented him from working or doing anything that was outside of the home. When she was concerned about him, Callie would take her home to attend to him during lunch break. Callie loved every minute of it because the co-worker was so kind, so gentle.

During the winter, when Callie went to her home, she offered Callie soup. It was very tasty, so Callie asked, "What kind of soup is this?" She said, "It's chicken noodle soup." Callie wanted to know how she made it. She showed Callie the can. Callie had never eaten chicken noodle soup from a can, only homemade. From that point forward, Callie always kept that brand of chicken noodle soup for a quick meal. It was economical, three to four cans for one dollar.

Okay, so Callie worked at the flower shop for the winter break while she continued to look for a full-time job. Eventually, she found one in an office with the Credit Bureau. She worked full time and she was fortunate to love her work. Her work schedule was one p.m. to nine p.m. Monday through Friday. She really did not have time for extensive periods of study for her classes after she had begun working full-time. She went to school in the morning and went to work in the afternoon. Her job required that she be on the telephone answering questions most of the time and a smaller part of time was dedicated to data entry.

Working at the credit bureau helped Callie to understand how credit worked. To be honest, Callie was not as astute as she could have been when it applied her. After working one year at the Credit Bureau, Callie would keep excellent credit for only five years.

Chapter 6: Plenty of Firsts

While in line to register for her classes, Callie introduced herself to a young lady named Bella. Callie asked her if she were going to stay on campus and Bella said, "I don't think that dormitories are available." Callie asked, "Do you live in Atlanta? She said, "Yes." Then, Callie asked, "Will you live at home, or will you get an apartment?" She said, "I don't know." Callie knew her every bit of five minutes when she asked, "Would you like to share an apartment with me?" Bella said, "yes."

They looked for an apartment that was close to campus and signed a lease. This was Callie's first apartment, and she was now living on her own. The apartment complex had lots of activities, which gave them an opportunity to be entertained without spending a lot of money. It was a beautiful apartment with beautiful surroundings. Callie and Bella shared everything. Callie went home with Bella and Bella went home to Clausell with Callie. They got along very well being that they only knew each other for a brief time before they moved in together.

After class, Bella went over to the clubhouse to play a game of pool. When she returned, she told Callie she met a lady that was very nice. Bella said that this lady was separated from her husband. She needed a roommate, so Bella presented the idea of getting a three-bedroom apartment, splitting the rent three ways. The rent for a two-bedroom apartment including utilities was two hundred and sixty-five dollars per month. Callie suggested to Bella, "Let's meet to talk about living together before we consider looking for a place and moving her in with us."

They all met to discuss the idea of splitting the rent three ways. Anna explained why she had separated from her husband and was seeking a divorce. She said, "I think he had another woman. So, I found another man to talk to about my problems. When I told my husband, he became violent and physically put me out of my house. He has not let me see my children. I left the city so that I can find a job and eventually get my children back." Although Anna was not who Callie expected, Callie's heart was sad for her. She asked, "How old are your children?" She told Callie, "They are eight, five and one, two boys and one girl." Callie's next question was, "How old are you? She answered, "Thirty." Thirty seemed so old to Callie.

Bella and Callie decided that they would share an apartment with Anna. The only challenge was that there were no three-bedroom apartments available in the complex where they lived. They would have to move out of the beautiful complex with all the amenities they enjoyed. The new apartment that they found did not have any amenities. The rent was the same amount as what they had paid for a two bedroom, two hundred and sixty-five dollars. Each of them would pay eighty-eight dollars and thirty-three cents and those included utilities. This was an opportunity for Callie to reduce the number of hours that she worked.

So, Callie Called Maria to let her know that she would be moving to a larger apartment. Maria then said, "Great! Come get your piano." Callie had no way to get her piano. She really wanted it; although, she acted as if it did not matter when Maria insisted: "If you don't come to get it, I am going to sell it or give it away." Callie would not let that interrupt her focus. Callie responded, "Just sell it Momma. Do whatever you want with it." Callie also told Maria to tell Raoul he can keep her car. Isn't that something? He already had it. Telling Maria that Raoul could keep her car gave Callie control. Silly. Nonetheless, it worked. That was a critical moment for Callie. Callie was never able to buy another piano though. Not only was Callie not able to buy another piano, Callie stopped playing the piano altogether.

In the meantime, her freshman year presented challenges that Callie was not equipped to handle alone. Still, she managed to do so. Callie wanted to ask her uncle for assistance. She knew she couldn't, knowing that her daddy was still trying all kind of ways to get her to come back to Clausell. Callie could not risk her parents telling her, as they had before: "A small-town girl does not know what it is like to live in the real world." Callie feared that they would come to Atlanta with a court order suggesting that she was mentally incapacitated and try to take her back to Monroeville. Raoul would try anything.

Her first incident occurred when she was going to her apartment. Callie was making a left turn into the apartment complex, where they lived. As she put on her signal to get into the turning lane, she got halfway through the lane and Bam! Suddenly, Callie was hit in the rear of her car. The impact of the accident dazed Callie. Her neck jerked, and her body went through this jolt that made Callie feel very weird. She had never been in a car accident, and she did not know what to do.

She looked in her rear-view mirror. This guy was getting out of his wrecked car, and he was about six feet, three inches tall, big and athletic looking. He yelled at Callie, "What are you doing? Look what you made me do! Why were you driving so slow?" Callie burst into tears: "I was getting into the turning lane to make a left; so, I could go home!" Fortunately, Callie was driving on a well-traveled street. She got out of her car to look at the damage when the driver in a brand-new car kept making accusations. Callie shut down because she was trying to figure out what should her first step be, knowing that she was supposed to be at work in a couple of hours. The policeman came and took their statements. Callie received the document showing the date and time when she was to appear in court.

The other driver was annoyed with Callie instead of being thankful that he was alive, and that Callie appeared to be uninjured. Instead of retaliating with unkind words, Callie got into her bent-up car and drove to her apartment. She was sick for the next few days. The impact was so hard that it started her monthly cycle. It was nearing the time to go to court. Callie was scared and inexperienced. This was her first time going before a judge. Callie asked her friend from college to go with her. When they got to the courtroom, the guy that had hit her, approached the judge with fake pictures! The police officer who had written the citation to the big guy was not present.

When Callie saw what this dude was trying to do, the only experience Callie had was what she had seen on the Perry Mason television series. She mouthed, "Your honor that did not happen the way he said it happened." Callie asked the judge, "Do you have a few pencils that I can use to demonstrate what happened?" She handed Callie four pencils. Callie made another request, "I need a total of six pencils please." The judge gave her two more. Continuing,

Callie asked, "Your Honor, may I place them here?" Callie was referring to the space near the judge's gavel. She said, "Yes, you may." Callie explained, "These six pencils represent three lanes. The first lane is the turning lane. The next lane is the lane where I was driving. The third lane represents the lane closest to the sidewalk."

Callie went on to say to her, "I put my left signal light on to get into the turning lane. Before I could get all the way into the turning lane, he hit the part of my car that was still in the other lane." Callie assured her, "My car is beige. It is not green. Those pictures are not of my car." After the judge asked the guy a few more questions, she could discern that he had made some inconsistent statements or in shorter terms: He lied.

The judge then turned to Callie and asked, "What damages are you seeking?" Callie informed her that she had gotten estimates and all she wanted was her car repaired for a little under four hundred dollars. The judge inquired, "Are you sure that is all you are seeking?" Callie confirmed, "Yes." The judge ordered him to pay for her damages.

Callie and her friend were ecstatic. Callie had appeared in court for the first time and won her first court case concerning her first car accident. Callie told her uncle after it was all over. He said, "Callie that was crazy. You could have received more damages. His car was totaled. That means that the impact was very severe. Just because you did not go to the doctor does not mean you might not have problems later." Further he said, "What about your lost wages." Callie said, "Well, I am just happy it is over." He said, "Why didn't you tell me what was going on?" Callie told him, "I was afraid you would tell momma and daddy." He ended the conversation by saying, "Callie, you should have told me."

Another first for Callie occurred near the end of her freshman year. She loved to swim; nevertheless, she had learned how to swim from the lifeguard at the local swimming pool in Clausell when she was fifteen years old. She registered for a swimming class in college to learn proper techniques. The students were taking their final exam for the swimming class. Callie was third in line. When she completed the pool part of the exam, she got out of the water and headed to the locker room to shower because she needed to be at work by one p.m.

On her way to the locker room, Callie met a female classmate that had just taken her pool examination. She was walking toward Callie and as soon as she met up with Callie, she blurted out, "There is a man in the locker room." Callie looked at her. "Really? Maybe one of the male students went into the locker room by mistake." Disagreeing with her, Callie's classmate said, "Oh, I don't know about that. I don't think so." They decided to walk back to the shower together.

As Callie was talking and walking with her, Callie whispered, "Where in the locker room did you see him?" She said, "He was going into the first shower stall." They went in together. They looked inside the first shower stall. No one was there. Callie felt that her reasoning was correct. A student must have gone in by mistake; so, the other student left.

Callie had to take a shower because she had to go to work after her class. To be safe, Callie went to the back of the shower section. She wanted to make sure that if a male student entered by mistake again, surely, he would recognize it by the time he went further into the locker room. When Callie went into the last shower stall, a white male was standing in the shower with his pants down. Callie yelled, turned and started running. She must have scared him. He started running too. Callie thought that he was running after her. On her way out, she tripped on one of the benches in the locker room and fell. He ran past her. Callie got up and started running toward the swimming pool in the opposite direction. Callie never looked back.

Callie was soft spoken. That day Callie used a lot of energy yelling. She was yelling for Miss Able. There was a long hallway to the pool and Callie ran all the way down that hallway yelling for Miss Able. Callie screamed, "Miss Able! Miss Able! A man is in the locker room with his pants down!" Callie was talking fast. Ms. Able said, "What?" By then Callie had made it all the way to the swimming pool. Callie said, "Miss Able! There was a man in the locker room shower with his pants down!" The swimming area had windows all around. Through her peripheral vision, a person caught Callie's attention running on the outside of the building alongside the windows of the swimming pool area. Callie pointed and yelled, "And there he is!"

It was raining outside. The guys, who were standing around, were waiting to take the test. One male student who was in the pool taking his test jumped out and started running with Callie's other male classmates after the man that was in the locker room. Callie was the only Black person in the class. Still, everyone was trying to either catch him or comfort her. She was noticeably rattled, so she stayed in the pool area until she was summoned to go to the administrative office area. The male classmates that had run after the man finally caught him. Security took over from there. Those classmates returned to the swimming area and showed others what they did to catch him. They got a thrill explaining it. Callie was silent while trying to process what had occurred.

When Callie arrived at the school's administrative offices, she saw the Dean, a Policeman, and a pregnant white lady huddled in the area outside of the office. The Policeman told Callie that the man in the locker room had escaped from the nearby mental institution. The pregnant white lady was his wife. Callie looked at her. She was thin with mousy colored brown hair and a big stomach, ready to deliver any moment. Callie should have been thinking about herself and the injury she had sustained; still, she was concerned for her.

The policeman and the Dean were asking Callie questions. With only her towel over her wet swimsuit, Callie answered their questions. One question was what happened in the locker room? Callie told them, "When I went in to take my shower after I finished my test, there was a man with this mans pulled down to the floor, standing in the shower stall. I turned to run away from him, and I tripped on the bench in the locker room, and I fell."

Callie did not tell them that she hurt her ribs when she fell. They told Callie that the mental patient was no threat. Furthermore, the police officer quoted the mental patient who said, "I just had to use the bathroom." Callie was listening carefully. She didn't say anything after the officer communicated the mental institution patient's statement. The officer continued, "He was not trying to hurt anyone." The Dean asked, "Would you like to go to the doctor?" She said, "No. I am okay." Although Callie knew she was hurt, she declined the offer because she thought she had to pay for it. She had no medical insurance, and her money was limited. Besides that, she was thinking about getting to work on time. Then the police officer asked, "Would you like to press charges against him?" Callie looked at the intruder's pitiful, pregnant wife and mumbled, "No." Again, Callie did not tell her parents or her uncle what she had experienced.

Sharing an apartment with Anna was fun until Anna met this guy who was not a law-abiding citizen. Callie did not know that at the time. She and Bella used to tease her about having a sugar daddy. They had heard about sugar daddies. Neither one of the girls really knew what a sugar daddy meant. Callie thought a sugar daddy was a boyfriend who was old enough to be your daddy. So, if Anna was thirty years old, he was fifty years old. Any way you slice it, he was not a good influence on Anna or Bella and Callie for that matter. Since Callie and Bella were in school, their association with them, however, was limited.

Too many times, when Callie came home from school, there were different people of questionable character around. She would just go into her room and close the door. Bella eventually sat out a quarter from school. Callie did not try to reprimand her or anything because she thought that it would only be for one quarter. Just stressed to the hilt, Bella wanted to go out for a night of fun and asked if Callie would like to go with them. Callie decided to go with Bella, Anna and her boyfriend for a drink in downtown Atlanta. The legal age for drinking then was eighteen years old.

Within minutes of arriving at the bar, Anna and her boyfriend disappeared. Callie asked Bella where they had gone. She said, "I think that they are in the back gambling." Callie raised up, looking dumbfounded, she inquired, "Gambling?" Bella laughed. They often talked about how green Callie was when it came to life. Callie paid them no attention and she knew it was a matter of time before she would be the brunt of their jokes.

Callie was curious after more time passed. She asked Bella to show her where Anna and her boyfriend were. Then something incredible occurred. Another first for Callie was when the wall opened when Bella knocked on it. Behind the wall, there were tables and chairs with people sitting around them playing cards. On closer examination, they were gambling. Callie knew there was illegal activity going on and did not want to be present if there were a raid. She knew that much from watching television shows.

Seriously, a lot of stuff that Callie had learned came from watching television. She asked Bella if they could leave, but they decided to wait patiently for Anna and her boyfriend to finish playing cards. Once they finished, Callie had decided in her heart that she would not go anywhere with them again.

On Friday afternoon of that same week, a letter was taped to the door when Callie came home early from school. Just as Callie was removing the letter from the door, the telephone rang. It was the telephone company and the customer service representative asked to speak to Callie Clausell. Curiously, she answered, "This is Callie."

The representative asked her several questions, one question of which was perplexing. The representative asked, "Are you running a business from your apartment? "Callie replied, "No! Why do you ask? Is something wrong?" The customer service rep said, "We have noticed that there is a lot of activity on this number." Callie was inquisitive: "What kind of activity?" The telephone company representative answered, "There are over two hundred calls that are placed from your number per week."

In a defensive manner, Callie countered, "It cain't be. I am in school during the day. I just came home early today because I did not have to work." The agent's response was the telephone company would continue to watch the line and if the high volume of calls continued, they would have to change the rate.

After the phone call, Callie went straight to Bella's room to find out if she had any answers. Bella never left her bedroom door open; yet it was wide open. Callie called her name before she walked into the room to look around. As she walked in, she noticed that a small plastic bag was on her well-made up bed. She was curious about the contents of the bag, for she had been suspicious about the different people that had frequented the apartment. Thus, she picked up the bag, opened it, smelled what was inside, then stuck her finger into the bag to taste it. Her tongue tingled; so, it could not have been sugar, nor salt, and certainly not flour because she was familiar with the taste of those items. What other alternative could there be? It may have been a drug, cocaine. Callie put the bag back on the bed and waited in the living room for Bella to come home.

Before Callie discovered the drugs on Bella's bed, she was thinking about the reason for the call from the telephone company. Still concerned about what had just occurred, she was subconsciously rolling up a paper in her hand when she recognized it was the letter that was attached to the front door. She read the letter only to learn that it was an eviction notice. Callie had gone from troubled to fierce.

Hours passed before Bella came home. When Bella walked into the apartment, Callie tried to control her anger as her head was about to explode. Biting the inside of her jaw to release the pressure, Callie could calmly ask Bella about the call from the telephone company. Bella exposed Anna and her boyfriend saying, "They are running a gambling business. That is why there were so many calls. I did not want to tell you because I knew you would get very nervous like when we went downtown to the bar."

Callie was not sure of the extent of the gambling. At that time, it wasn't a priority. She wanted to move on with getting an explanation about the bag on the bed, asking Bella, "Why was there a plastic bag on your bed with white stuff in it? You left your bedroom door opened; so, as I walked in, I saw this bag on your bed.

Bella dropped her head in shame: "It belongs to me. Anna gave it to me for keeping a secret about the gambling. It's cocaine. I was going to sell it because I needed some money." Callie said, "Money? Why Bella do you need money? Our expenses are low. Why?" Her gloomy eyes met Callie's eyes and she confessed: "I had lost some money gambling. It was a few dollars here and there, nothing big. But then, I got addicted and could not stop because I was hoping to win."

Callie sighed, "Oh Bella, I appreciate your honesty. Why did you wait to tell me? We have been so close. Is that why we are receiving an eviction notice?" Callie felt sorry for Bella because prior to Anna becoming a roommate, they had enjoyed a good relationship. Therefore, Callie expressed herself with these words, "Bella, I have tried my best not to judge you or Anna. I will not live like this. I am not a criminal and I do not want to be around people that involve themselves with criminal activity. I do not want to go to jail. I am leaving tonight." Bella said nothing else as Callie picked up the telephone to call her uncle.

Callie knew then that this was much bigger than she could handle, so she called Uncle Javier, a first time for calling him and asked: "Can I please store my stuff in your garage until I can get a place to live? Uncle Javier, I need help." He said, "What's wrong?" Callie told him the entire story. He comforted her when he said, "You can stay here Callie." Although he had more than enough space in his house for Callie, she knew she had outgrown the arrangement of living with them. She needed her own space; although, she agreed to stay for a few days. Callie left her apartment that night.

For whatever strange reason, Callie stayed focused after she left her apartment. She spoke with her friends at school that were her neighbors about the reason she had left her apartment abruptly. They surprised Callie with more information about her ex-roommates. They had been evicted and all their stuff was outside. It took place sooner than Callie thought it would happen. Just imagine if she had not come home early from school to retrieve the eviction notice, her precious few items would have been placed outside for the scavengers. Also, imagine how that eviction would have affected her credit and the ability to have purchasing power. Callie was still concerned about that because her name was on the lease. Would she be responsible for any remaining additional costs?

A week had passed living with Uncle Javier and Callie was concerned about where she would live. Her old place was convenient to school. She just had too much going on to try to find somewhere else to live. When Callie expressed her concerns to her uncle, he said, "Go back to management at the apartment where you lived. Explain to them what developed. They may give you an apartment and not report you to the credit bureau."

It was good advice and Callie was glad that she confided in her uncle and followed his advice. Callie explained to management why she left abruptly. The resident manager granted her request to get another apartment without paying a security deposit. They did not report it to the credit bureau. Neither did she incur other costs. It all worked out.

Although initially, Callie was angry with Bella and Anna, Callie began to remember how Bella and Callie had gotten alone without any drama, specifically, before Anna entered the picture. Callie re-established contact with Bella.

Bella separated from Anna and ended up getting married. She did not graduate from college. Anna and her boyfriend went to jail. They were sentenced to five years for credit card fraud.

Callie felt that God had protected her. She had always believed in God, even though, she did not attend church often. Callie could have been declared guilty by association. She was happy that she acted quickly to separate herself from bad association.

Those unpleasant incidents were first-time encounters that happened while Callie was trying to make a life for herself. They were significant being that Callie did not have the experience needed to handle them; yet somehow, she made it through the tribulations. However, not quitting in those situations gave Callie depth.

At some point, Callie decided to drive the car she had bought from her uncle to Clausell. When Callie got home, she did not expect that her daddy would still be holding a grudge. She had predicted that her daddy would give her a tough time. He did not speak directly to her at all, only through Maria. How insane? Even though she dealt with his controlling childish behavior, it was only because she knew her trip was for a weekend. Right in front of Callie, he instructed Maria to tell Callie this, "You should not be driving this car because the tires are really worn, and you could have an accident." He was right, anything could happen. Somehow his unbelievable pride kept him from helping his daughter when she needed it.

Callie worked hard to pay for her apartment and college. She could receive some financial support for college through one of the college programs. Categorically, the out-of-state fees were monstrous. Her freshman year was financially difficult; though, Callie would not apply for a student loan.

Since she was attending a community college, her loan would not have been astronomical. Yet, the timing of getting one, would have been too much for her; even though, she had no overwhelming debt at that time. So, she decided to suffer through it for one year. By then, she would have become a resident. To Callie, having that debt would have been like eating one meal and paying for it the rest of her life.

She would sacrifice eating rather than going into debt while in college. About three days before Callie would get her paycheck, she ran out of food. She had no extra money, and she was hungry. Her friends were out of town. She could not write a check because she only had enough money for her bills. Never would Callie try to get money by writing checks if the money were not in the bank. At that time, she had never returned a check or as the saying was in the South, bounced a check.

As Callie was driving through a little strip mall near her apartment and meditating on how to solve her problem, she spotted a big trailer that had signs posted. One sign read, "Give us your opinion." Callie decided to stop to see what it was all about. The company wanted potential customers to complete a survey on shopping. After completing the survey, they would give the participant money. Callie completed the survey and received her two-dollar food certificate that she used to buy food items.

She bought twelve eggs and a box of grits. She had salt and pepper packets which she had received with her fast-food orders. She kept those packets for challenging times, and it paid off. Because she knew how to cook, she could stretch her money and it always helped Callie out financially. Although things looked grim at times, it did not break Callie because she was living her dream, to live in Atlanta. She had hope because she kept this saying close to her heart: "When you have hope, you are not broke."

Maria did what she could to help Callie when she visited Monroeville. She would consistently pack a box of food and send it back with Callie, a tremendous help. Callie had almost completed her freshman year on this visit and although Raoul was still pouting, he decided to leave four hundred dollars on the corner of the dining room table with a message he gave to Maria to deliver to Callie.

She said, "Callie, your daddy left you four hundred dollars to buy some tires for your car." The gesture exasperated Callie: "Momma, when I needed the help, he would not help me. He doesn't talk to me. He took my car that I paid for, and I let him. I don't want his help." Callie did not take the money. She left it there on the table and drove back to Atlanta.

Callie had completed her freshman year and now it was summer. She made another weekend visit to Clausell.

Again, her dad left money on the corner of the table with a message from another family member, one of her sisters. Her sister reasoned with Callie, saying, "Callie, just take the money and leave. He is trying to apologize the best way he knows how." When Callie considered her sister's eyes, she felt pity for her. She recognized that she would be no better than her daddy, if she did not forgive him. And now she has an onlooker, her sister who could be deeply affected. Subsequently, Callie took the money and left.

Shortly before the fall semester was about to begin, Callie went back to Monroeville to bring one of her sisters for a few weeks to visit. Her sister had gotten a little homesick while in Atlanta and missed her friends. She wanted to go home. Callie told her that she did not have any money to go to Monroeville. Her sister said, "Callie, it's just gas." Callie told her again, she just did not have enough money.

A few days later, while Callie was at work, her sister had been listening to the radio. She called, "Callie, I heard about a swimsuit competition, and they are paying fifty dollars if you win. You can participate and win the money and take me home." Callie laughed and said, "A swimsuit competition? That's a lot of money just to walk around in a swimsuit for a few minutes. I can't do that." Her sixteen-year-old sister said, "Yes you can." Callie felt sorry for her sister, so she changed her mind, "Okay, I will do it. What if I don't win? I have never done anything like this ever." Begging Callie and at the same time showing confidence in Callie, she said, "Come on. Please. You can win. You will win. Do you promise you will take me home if you win?" Callie made an agreement: If I win, I promise to take you home. If I don't win, you will have to wait until I get some money."

It would be another first for Callie. She asked about four of her friends from college to come along for moral support. Since her sister had suggested it, she took her along too. Callie did not know what to expect. It was in a very popular, well-advertised night club. Yes, a nightclub. She was extremely nervous when she got there, then she mustered up the courage to ask what she needed to do to be included in the competition. The competition began at ten p.m. The club manager instructed the girls where to walk and stand. The crowd's applause decided who would be the winner.

The contestants were all in this small room where each contestant came out one by one. Callie heard the applause for the other ladies that went before her, and finally, it was her turn. Callie loved yellow and she wore a simple two-piece yellow swimsuit with a bow on each side of the bottom. It was very cute for a thirteen-year-old. Obviously, cute was in then. The applause for Callie seemed loud to her. Then again because she was nervous, it was difficult to tell who the winner was. All the contestants were on the floor, side by side in front of a glaring crowd.

The master of ceremonies asked for another round of applause for each of the contestants as he walked by, putting his hand over each contestant's head while signaling for the crowd's applause. When he walked by Callie, the crowd went into a roar. Yes, low and behold, Callie won. She could not believe it. Callie took the money and ran. The contest was held on Wednesday, and they left for Monroeville Friday after Callie finished work.

When they reached Monroeville, the girls excitedly told Maria what had happened. Maria could not believe it. She unexpectedly asked, "Callie, you took your sister to a night club? Callie told her, "Yes, momma. She was the one who believed I could win. So, I wanted her to see it. I was scared, but apart from that, it was exciting." Maria stayed quiet because she saw how happy her girls were and she was happy to see them happy.

Chapter 7: Debt Became Master

Callie never had a concrete plan of what she would do with her life. She just got as far as going to Atlanta. She had a lot of interests. Unfortunately, nothing stood out to her. If you recall, Callie rebelled against taking accounting in high school her senior year. Her rebellion was short lived because she ended up doing very well in accounting.

With that boost in confidence, Callie decided to major in accounting at the community college she attended. Her first accounting class in college was horrible. Callie did not want to withdraw from her class because she felt that everything would work out, that she would catch on and catch up. For that reason, she waited too long to withdraw from the class and when she withdrew, she had a failing grade, so instead of receiving a "W" she received a "WF" on her transcript which was not good for her grade point average.

If over half of the class had not failed, Callie might have thought it was just her misfortune. But in this case, it was the teacher who was incompetent and having trouble teaching her very first class. She was fired. Her replacement was an older more experienced professor, so Callie retook the class and received a "B."

In this class, Callie learned something from her professor that she had not known before. As her professor passed out the exams, he said, "This student does not ever need to put her name on her paper." Callie listened carefully as he continued: "She's the only one in the class who makes her check marks backwards, Callie Clausell."

Callie reached for her paper to see what he was talking about. She did not see what he was talking about, as Callie had always made them that way. The shortest part of the check mark was on the right side and the longest part of the check mark was on the left side. He had to point that out to her. Anyhow, being left-handed in those days was not easy. Callie was used to getting to class early just to get one of the two desks for left-handed people, so that her arm would not hang in air without support while she was writing.

It was getting closer to the time for Callie to graduate. As it stood, she needed one more class, cost accounting, to graduate with an Associate's degree in Accounting. The problem was that this class would not be offered again until the following year. Guess what Callie did? She changed her major to Business Administration. Then she asked the Dean if he would allow her to use one of her electives as a core class so that she could graduate and start working in her field. Callie explained that she could not wait an entire year.

The Dean denied her request: "No, you cannot use an elective as a core class." Callie came back the next day to ask him again. Again, he said, "No, Miss Clausell. That is out of the question." Callie came back the next day and out of frustration he reiterated with a whisper: "No, I am not going to approve this." He was very familiar with Callie because she had taken his economics class.

Callie put on her negotiation cap that she had perfected. She reasoned with him. "What is it to you? It's one class, five hours." He just looked at her for a long time, then said: "No, I am not approving your request." She was relentless. "Okay, I will come back every day to see you until you change your mind." This went on for about four weeks.

He started to get really irritated with Callie. He learned that she was not about to quit. Then this cinched the deal. She said, "Okay, if you sign this release for me to graduate, I will not bother you again. And furthermore, I will never return to the school. I promise." He signed the release. Callie graduated and never went back.

Her sister started attending the community college where Callie had graduated. Many of her professors recognized her last name and asked if she knew Callie Clausell. She said, "We are sisters." She was so wound up because the accounting professor gave Callie a compliment for being a good student.

Also, another Dean in Admissions wanted to know why Callie did not return to school events such as homecoming, since Callie had been on the homecoming court. Her sister couldn't answer and when she asked Callie why she didn't come to school events, Callie answered, "I have outgrown that. Don't have time." She at no time told her sister the reason.

Callie attended a community college because she was not interested in attending a four-year university that she could not afford and that could not guarantee that she would get a fantastic job. She said, "Would the degree be worth the debt." Callie wanted to graduate within the two-year period and start a prosperous financial life. Part of her curriculum included taking income tax accounting which after completing this class and before graduating, she approached Uncle Javier to help her buy a house. He could not believe it: "Are you sure?"

Callie informed him that she was sure and gave him the reason why she was prepared to buy a house. The tax accounting class she had taken gave her valuable insight on how she could benefit herself by purchasing a house. He showed Callie a two-bedroom brick house which was a foreclosure. There were new hardwood floors throughout and a full basement on about one half-acre of land. That was the house for Callie.

She purchased the house at nineteen years old. It cost twenty-five thousand dollars. Her mortgage would be two hundred and twenty-five dollars per month for thirty years. Her parents could not imagine Callie paying two hundred and twenty-five dollars for a mortgage, although her rent used to be more. Perhaps, it was because their mortgage was one hundred and thirty-five dollars for a new house. Callie explained to Maria that the cost of living was higher in Atlanta than in Monroeville.

Callie had bought some furniture when she was living with her roommates; so, all Callie needed was kitchen appliances and a bedroom suite for the extra bedroom. Maria was excited for Callie, and she found a used refrigerator and stove for a great price. She got Raoul to come with her to bring it to Callie. Sometimes people just need time to manage change.

Almost two years had gone by since Callie left, Monroeville and Raoul had finally gotten over his bitterness about Callie leaving home. Not long after Raoul and Maria brought the appliances to Callie, they returned to pay a surprise visit to Callie and her sister. The sisters had decided to have a sale of all their old clothes. They were nice clothes.

They had washed them, pressed them, folded them and put price tags on all the items. The sisters felt that they would not have any problems selling the clothes because Callie's house was in a convenient location for passersby to see.

About an hour into the sale, a blue ford LTD was coming toward the house. There was a little island that divided the main highway from her street. The sisters watched in shock as the car came closer and closer, then pulled into the driveway. It was Raoul and Maria. In any event, when Raoul got out of the car, he walked over to the table, looked around and picked up an item. Then he asked, "What are you girls doing?" Excitedly, Callie answered, "We are having a sale of the clothes that we do not want anymore."

If you know anything about the television show, Beverly Hillbillies, characters named Granny and Jed always came up with off-the-wall comments. Raoul was no different. Even if he did not say anything, his expression spoke volumes. The bottom line was that he did not buy their explanation. Raoul thought they needed the money, and they did not want to ask them for it. Here they were in the public's view on the corner of a moderately busy street selling second-hand clothes, or in his mind's eye begging.

They explained more fully that they were having fun knowing that they could make money off items they no longer wanted or needed. His next question was, "How much money do you expect to make at this here sale?" They said, "About two hundred dollars." He reached into his back pocket and pulled out his wallet, opened it and took out two crisp one hundred dollars bills that looked like he had ironed them with spray starch. He looked at each of his daughters, then handed one hundred dollars to each girl of which each accepted. Next, he asked them to bag up all the clothes. They bagged up the clothes and handed the clothes to Maria to place in the car.

Raoul and Maria did not even come inside the house. What they saw was too much for them to bear. They visited outside for about twenty minutes, and they went back to Monroeville.

Later, Maria told Callie that Raoul gave the clothes away when he returned to Monroeville. Basically, from Maria's comments, she felt that Raoul was embarrassed. To him, it appeared that they were begging and everyone in the community would hear about it. Maybe so, if the sisters had that sale in Clausell because no one had yard sales in Clausell. But Atlanta? No one in Callie's neighborhood knew Raoul. It was somewhat hypocritical for Raoul to express so much pride when he had no shame when it came to his drinking binges that were well known in Clausell. Taking into consideration Raoul's feelings, Callie never had a yard sale again.

Although Callie purchased the house for a tax break, she did not bargain on receiving all the other credit cards in the mail. She was puzzled about receiving the cards, since she had not applied for any. After the purchase of the house, Callie received credit cards from Sears, JC Penny and Visa. When Callie told her workmates, one of them retorted, "I am older than you are. I applied for a Sears Card and never received one. What did you do to get it?" Callie said, "Maybe it was because I purchased a house." Callie had worked for the Credit Bureau her freshman year in college. Because of that job, she had a basic understanding of credit and assumed the purchase boosted her credit.

Uncle Javier gave Callie tidbits of advice from time to time concerning building credit. When Callie got her first credit card, he recommended, "Pay your bills on time or early; and eventually, the store will increase your credit limit." Callie did well with that, and in time as he said, her credit limited was raised. Her first credit card had a limit of two hundred dollars. Within two years, her credit limit had jumped to two thousand dollars for one revolving account and ten thousand dollars for an installment account.

Her credit was excellent, but Callie was not prepared for the word debt again. She had heartaches and countless challenges. Many times, she felt that she was all alone. It was like she expected and accepted that feeling because she was growing and experiencing life, something she had to do alone.

After graduation, Callie's financial aid advisor recommended her for a position with the District Office for the Community College where Callie graduated. Callie interviewed and got the job with the primary responsibility of purchasing for the two campuses as well as paying invoices. Life got sweeter.

Her income was quite large for a twenty-year-old, who was the youngest of the entire staff. Within a brief time, Callie now had five Visa cards. The cards allowed her to look as if her net worth were more than it essentially was. Credit cards had given Callie a false sense of security. The discipline she once had was slowly disappearing like a mist. Callie learned that giving credit cards to an undisciplined person was like giving a little child a pack of candy and expecting the child to take one piece and put the rest away. Callie noticed that she, as well as other friends, was living on credit cards. Here is another behavior that Callie noticed but was unable to control. Once she made a purchase with the card, she kept purchasing because it was easy. When she paid with cash, her purchases were fewer. Callie had not yet gotten into serious financial trouble; and therefore, she was able to make all of her payments on time.

Well-meaning friends thought that all Callie was missing in her life was being in a committed relationship. Her best friend and the best friend's boyfriend thought they would set up a blind date for Callie and that they could all go out for a nice evening. When Callie popped in that night to meet the young man, he was sitting down in her friend's dimly lit apartment in all black attire. He had on a black hat, black shirt, black pants, black shoes and dark sunglasses. Callie wondered if he was blind, not that she had anything against blind people. He was suspicious looking and not quite the type of person Callie would want to be alone with or for that matter go on a double date.

Without a second thought, she at once made up an excuse, while politely thanking her friends and the young man. She said, "I would not have thought of canceling on the phone. I came over to meet you in person and offer my sincere apology for not being available to go on a date." Remember, all in her family could have been award winning actors. Callie added, "My sister had an emergency, and she is waiting for me to pick her up. She had an accident and cannot drive her car." Of course, Callie lied. You would have too if you had seen this man!

A few weeks passed, and the same friends wanted to introduce Callie to another guy. Callie declared, "No way!" Callie's best friend's boyfriend insisted that it would be a great match. Callie verbalized this, "I will meet him when your girlfriend meets him." Well, his girlfriend, Callie's best friend met him, leaped for joy and called Callie. She said,

"Girl, he's okay! Get dressed!" This time Callie selected a public place just in case she needed to escape again. Since she had to shampoo her hair and finish it, it took a lot longer for her to get there. She made it by eleven p.m.

It appeared to be a perfect match, the missing part that her friends had convinced her that she needed. Callie had the degree, the house, the car, fantastic credit and now she had the man, the so-called American dream. But this relationship is what got Callie into debt. Almost four years into the relationship, he decided that he did not want any responsibilities any longer including being with Callie.

Callie made more money than he did and everything in the relationship belonged to her. He had no material advantages, and he created more bills without the income to support his purchases. Although he made donations to the bills that he had gotten while they were a couple, he decided that he did not want to make any more payments after they split. As a co-signer on all his purchases, Callie was left holding the bag. He yelled, "I am not going to give you anything!" He left Callie with D-E–B–T.

There Callie was twenty-four years old and in insurmountable debt. Many of their friends thought he was going through a phase, and they would reconcile. Initially, Callie had hoped for that too. At any rate, that situation was more than Callie could handle. How could she trust him again? Left up to her, there would be no reconciliation. On many occasions, he had voiced his concerns about Callie owning everything. Why was that an issue later and not in the beginning of their relationship? What's more, when he left, he took her car. Out of spite, he kept it for several months. Callie did not know where it was. Since he had her car, she was still giving him the benefit of the doubt by thinking he would make the payments and do the right thing. He didn't make the payments, and neither would he return the car.

Trying to stay amiable was difficult after that went down. She had to bring out the fight in her to survive this catastrophe. No way to ignore this conflict. Callie had to threaten him with calling the police to report that her car was stolen. She knew where his momma lived. She informed his momma that she was going to press charges against him if he did not return her car. His momma got the message to him.

Instead of him taking the honorable approach to return the car, he called the bank that was financing the car, informed the bank that he was going to park the car in the parking lot of a local mall and then called his momma to tell her what he had done. She called Callie to let her know. By the time Callie got to the mall to get her car, the bank had already done so. When Callie contacted the bank to tell them what had occurred, she was informed that she would need to catch up all the past-due car payments, as well as what other fees it took to recover the car. She didn't have the money for that or for all the other bills that he had left for her to pay.

Callie traded in her old car to get this new expensive car. Now Callie did not have any car. Yes, the naive young woman lost two cars. Three if you count the one Raoul took. The whole thing had burned Callie badly. Her self-esteem was at an all-time low. One test that Callie would face in the future was would she trust another man to care for her and love her? Would Callie share what she had without prejudice? Would Callie become bitter and group all men in the same category as being shiftless or irresponsible?

She hoped that she would not let this madness affect her negatively forever. Only time would tell. Only when she was in the situation would Callie truly know how she would respond.

A pressing, inevitable question had to be answered. How would Callie pay all this debt? That was too much for her to emotionally digest. She always tried to keep her promises. She had never considered defaulting on a loan. This was such a conflict for her and having debt embarrassed her. What Callie had taken pride in once, was out of her reach, keeping her promise.

Since she was mentally incapable of making a sound decision, she went to an older acquaintance who was a financial advisor and asked how she should proceed. He said, "Contact all of your creditors and arrange to make smaller payments. Set a date and the amount you can pay each creditor. Then negotiate making a balloon payment to pay off the debt in full after a while." The acquaintance was very experienced with an MBA in Finance and was very specific on how to handle it.

At the time of the suggestion, Callie did not have the confidence that she could carry out his advice because now she was unemployed, and she was too embarrassed to tell her financial advisor. She acknowledged that she received good advice. One fact that Callie should not have ignored was listening to relatives who did not have her value system. They suggested that Callie file bankruptcy, the opposite of what her financial acquaintance had recommended. What appealed to Callie was the opportunity to have a fresh start. So, when her relatives told her, it gives you a chance to start over, that affected her from this angle. Specifically, she would not have the constant reminder of the mistake she had made. If she had thoroughly reviewed the pros and cons of each suggestion; perhaps, she would have made a different decision.

Although the court system would forgive the debt after ten years, Callie would possibly still have an emotional scar. And only God knew for how long. Taking the financial advisor's advice to pay the creditors in the manner mentioned may have been resolved in three to four years.

However, the monthly reminder was too much for dear Callie.

Some seasonal jobs that Callie held proved that she was honest and reliable. She worked at a bank as a teller, handled safe deposit boxes and gave administrative support for one bank Vice President. Callie worked in the credit department of a large department store, handling large amounts of cash. It would have been difficult to consider those types of jobs again now that Callie was in debt and was about to file bankruptcy. What an infectious disease!

Callie began working for a temp agency and received a few six-week assignments. Next, she needed to buy a car because some of her assignments were not on the bus line. Her sister knew a car salesman that sold Callie what they called in the country, a "plucker." It was what Callie could afford. It helped her to get around town. The car salesman knew her financial situation and worked out a payment plan. The payment was very small in comparison to the other car payment that Callie had. Eventually, Callie could pay it off.

Slowly but surely, Callie started to get a grip on life again. She reasoned that she needed a job with limited stress which in turn would allow her to work on herself. She wanted to find a job working from nine to five p.m. She wanted to have latitude to make decisions and manage the office while the boss was out of the office. After explaining to her sister what she wanted, her sister said, "Callie, where are you going to find a job like that?" Callie said, "It exists. I will find it."

Guess what? Callie found a job supporting the Vice President of Professional Education in a non-profit organization. It met her preliminary requirements, and she scheduled an interview that very day.

When Callie interviewed, she knew this was the job for her. She was candid during her interview because she had nothing to lose. In fact, Callie got along exceptionally well with her prospective employer. So much so, Callie got the job. The hours were from nine to five p.m. Callie understood the job requirements well and could perform them with no problems. Part of her responsibilities included keeping accurate records of continuing education for medical doctors, which allowed Callie to use her strong organizational skills. Her boss was very fair-minded. She knew that Callie worked diligently to finish a project, even if it meant working late. She had no problem instructing Callie to take some down time when needed if she were out of the office. Callie's boss trusted her, and this made Callie very happy.

Callie learned that sometimes all you need is one person to believe in you. She would have continued working there indefinitely if her boss had not accepted a position out of state. Callie needed to act while her confidence was alive and strong. With her boss' support, she applied for another job at a computer company and was hired. Her salary increased by six thousand dollars.

Chapter 8: Competition Was Valuable

Almost two years after Callie's disturbing debt crisis, she met a young man through another friend. Jason called to ask Callie and her sister if they would be preparing Thanksgiving dinner. Callie replied, "No, I had not planned on doing that." Jason went on to relate that he wanted to bring his *little baby brother* over to get him out of the house.

Callie spoke to her sister about it while holding the phone asking, "Hey Sis, do you want to cook today?" She said, "Yes!" She loved to cook. Callie responded to her friend, "Yes, that's ok." She told him that she had to run out to get a few items for the meal and that he and his *little baby brother* could watch the game with her family.

Callie was gone for over an hour trying to find a few things to complement the turkey she had in her freezer. When she drove up, there was a white Fiat in her parking space. She concluded that her friend's *little baby brother* must have been at least sixteen years old. She thought that because Jason drove a red BMW. This Fiat must have been the *little baby brother's* car.

Callie struggled to the door with her two medium size bags of groceries. As she unlocked the door, she almost dropped one of the bags when she looked up and saw a man sitting on her couch. He stood up. He was about six feet two inches tall, chiseled, cut, with no fat anywhere on his body. He was wearing a white t-shirt that gripped every muscle in his upper body. He had a midnight shadow showing that he had not shaven in a day or so. And if that were not enough, he quickly flashed a million-dollar smile. His teeth were white like snow and his smiled stretched from ear to ear on his square jawbone.

He walked toward Callie and gently grabbed the bag she was struggling with quite clumsily. As he took control of the bag, Callie stumbled through the words saying, "You are a man." For a second time, Callie said it with a little more force. With a puzzling, yet inquisitive tone in her voice, "You are a man." His sheepish smile made her feel that she had embarrassed him because surely there was no reason to think that he lacked self-confidence. Since she had spent so much time searching for food on a holiday for who she thought was going to be a little boy, she felt inclined to voice her surprise. Although Callie did not want to be rude to him, she wanted to let him know this fact that she could not bring herself to say out loud: "I would not have gone out looking for food to complement the turkey if I thought that you were a man. I was cooking because I thought that this *little baby brother* was a child or teenager."

It's been said that there are always two sides to a story. And this was his story. He was not embarrassed that Callie had uttered the words, "You are a man" a couple of times. He felt that she was flirting, and the seductiveness of her voice made him certain. She was breathless because of the struggle she had carrying the bags in without putting them down to unlock the door. Nothing more. Callie did not know what seductive was. She was just a small-town girl from Clausell that loved wearing a cut-off t-shirt, daisy duke shorts and flip-flops when she had company coming over. Most of the time she had the same attire on but without shoes. The words that Callie spoke twice, "You are a man" meant that she had not considered cooking for her adult siblings and parents, why would she consider cooking for an adult man that she did not know?

Possibly, Jason knew that too. Initially, when he asked if Callie and her sister were cooking for Thanksgiving, Callie said, "No." Being the subtle manipulator that he was, Jason tried to get her heart involved by asking, "Why don't you cook and let me bring my *little baby brother* over?" Masterful indeed. Certainly, unsuspecting to Callie. She had forgotten how good Jason was at pulling a person in and leading the person to the conclusion he wanted to achieve.

Callie ended up preparing the entire meal because her sister decided not to help for whatever reason. It may have been because the *little baby brother* directed his attention to Callie when she came in and she could not deal with it. By the time Callie's guests were prepared to eat, they all were just simply tired and famished. Dismissing the confusion, they all had a hearty meal that they enjoyed.

As a kind gesture to Callie for receiving Jason and his brother for dinner, the *little baby brother* who was an extra-large baby brother invited Callie and her sister to a party at the Fox Theatre the following Saturday, a couple of days after Thanksgiving. Callie was really impressed that the *little baby brother* acknowledged her kindness in such a grand way by extending an invitation, not only to her, but to her sister who was very temperamental and had not taken part in preparing the meal. Callie accepted the invitation with pleasure.

Callie had selected her entire outfit Saturday morning to wear to the Fox. Since it was a big event, she did her nails and hair. She noticed that her sister was not preparing for the evening out. She asked her, "Do you already know what you are going to wear?" Suddenly, her sister emotionally responded, "I am not going!" Callie repeated what she thought she heard, asking, "Did you say you are not going?" "That's correct." Disappointment was all over Callie's face, so she asked, "Why not?" "I just do not want to go."

Callie was troubled as she did not want to go alone. She started pleading with her sister to change her mind. Her sister gave no reason for her ungracious change of mind. Neither did she want to discuss it any further. Silence engulfed the entire household the rest of the day. Right before the telephone rang, Callie decided to ask her sister to reconsider her decision. "No. What did I tell you?" she yelled. Callie did not say anything in response.

About ten p.m., Callie's home telephone rang. She contemplated whether she should answer because she was now depressed. She did, and her mood quickly changed. It was her cousins, Jabot and Naomi who were on their way to Monroeville for a visit. Callie had found a solution. She could attend the party and be viewed as hospitable if she were able to pull it off. Callie asked her cousin, "Where exactly are you guys?"

She was so overjoyed to know that they had not passed the exit to the Fox Theatre. She gave them the directions to the Fox along with instructions to tell Pierre, Jason's *little baby brother*, that she was on her way without her sister, because her sister had changed her mind. And since she did not want to come alone, she asked her cousins who were passing through from out of town to wait for her there.

When Callie got near to the theater, she hoped parking would be relatively easy to find. As she turned left, there was a parking spot right on the corner from the Fox and she just pulled in without a problem. In her rush to get there, she had forgotten her invitation. She had to ask the attendant who was guarding the door to get Pierre, so she could come inside. Within a few minutes, Pierre walked up smiling and grabbed her like he had grabbed the bags of groceries, this time giving her a bear hug and added, "Wow! You look amazing!"

Instead of thanking him, Callie said, "You know I don't look this good all the time." While Callie thought she was being coy with him, Pierre later told Callie that he thought that she had a confidence problem. He was right about her if he were speaking a few years ago. But that night, Callie did not have one bit of low self-esteem issues. She wore a long sleeved, V-necked, fitted black jumpsuit that resembled a cat suit with black pumps and pearls. That was really a dress-up for her if you consider the daisy dukes and t-shirt, he saw her in only three days ago. Pierre looked like a GQ model. He had visited the barber and had a fresh haircut with a clean shave that made his skin took smoother than a baby's bottom. He wore a Black suit with a white shirt and black tie.

Callie thanked Pierre for allowing her cousins to attend his party. She explained that since her sister did not want to attend, she was hesitant about coming downtown alone. In other words, Callie knew that her cousins were on the lookout for her. Pierre said, "Oh, I did not mind at all. It was my pleasure. And I hope you all have an enjoyable time."

The party was exciting. There were lots of prominent people there. One person that Callie had been on a few dates with was there. When he saw Callie, he walked across the room and asked her, "Who invited you to this party?" Callie responded, "The host" and walked away to start mingling with the other guests. Her cousins, Jabot and Naomi, were thoroughly impressed with the guest list. They stayed at the party for about two hours.

Wanting to thank the host before she left, Callie looked for Pierre and found him employing excellent hospitality to his guests. She thanked him for his attentiveness to her family. Pierre asked for her telephone number, claiming, "I want to make sure that you arrive home safely." Callie was touched by his concern and gave him her number. He already knew that Callie felt insecure coming alone. It made sense that he would call to make sure that she arrived safely home. When her cousins left, Callie left.

Somehow Pierre called before Callie made it home. Her sister had left the note on her bed. Now, Callie was really affected by his follow through. Here Pierre was hosting a party of over two hundred guests, and he took the time to check to see if Callie made it home safely.

Callie called. He inquired why it took so long for her to return his call. She said, "You know you served appetizers and I was really hungry. Given that, I stopped by the supermarket on the way home to get some food to cook. I had not eaten anything substantial because I was waiting to eat at the party and by the end of the night, I was feeling a little sick." Callie was hungry and cooking an omelet would be fast, healthy and economical. She ended the conversation by thanking him again for his concern.

The next day, Callie received another call from Pierre. He wanted to prepare dinner for Callie and her sister. Callie could not believe that he would still consider inviting her sister after she was a no show at his party at the Fox. Of course, Callie accepted the invitation. Do you think her sister went?

No, she did not. Callie went alone. Callie met Pierre's roommate. All of them had a great dinner with pleasant conversation. The food was delicious. He prepared a T-Bone steak, with garlic creamed potatoes, sautéed green beans and a garden salad. Pierre offered Callie a mimosa.

She had never had one before. Since a mimosa is made with orange juice and champagne, Callie was hesitant to accept since she did not like orange juice. Being the appreciative guest, Callie accepted the mimosa and expressed, "I would like just a small amount please." After she drank it, she felt more comfortably asking him to change the drink by only giving her the champagne.

Pierre called the next day, the next day, and the next day. After then they started dating officially. As they got closer, they were inseparable. They went just about every place together. Callie was on a date with Pierre when she needed to run to the ladies' room. She bumped into the person that she had gone out with on a couple of dates. He was the same person she saw at the Fox. "Hello" he said. "Hello, I can't talk to you now." She said this as she passed him not breaking her stride to get to the ladies' room.

The minute Callie approached Pierre, he said, "One of the guys that I had invited to my party at the Fox asked me if I were dating you." Callie said, "Oh yes, was it the person that I told you I went on a couple of dates with? If so, I just literally ran into him. Pierre remarked, "Yes, it was the same person. I felt sorry for him." "Why?" she asked. Pierre smiled and said, "I told him he just did not know what he had." Callie smiled. Pierre added, "You know that's what I told him." Callie said, "You are kidding me. Did you really tell him that?" He said, "Yes." Flattered, she responded, "Thank you for your kindness." Pierre said, "It's true!"

Callie humbly related to Pierre, "It was not like he was overly interested in me." She continued, "Just watch this. It never fails. When a man feels that a woman is not going to wait around, especially when he sees her with someone else, he will try to rekindle the relationship. It's a pride thing."

True to her words, within a few days of her telling Pierre that, her sister said that the fellow Callie previously dated, stopped by just to say hello. When she told Callie that, Pierre was just dropping Callie off, and he heard what she told Callie. Her sister did that on purpose. She was trying to sabotage the new relationship. She wanted Callie to date the other guy because he was rich. Aware of her determination to break them up, Callie went into damage control mode. "Pierre don't worry. He will not be stopping by again." After she set the matter straight, he never stopped by again.

Pierre was a very godly conscience person, always talking about the Bible. Callie did not know a thing about the Bible, at least not anything worth talking about. Considering that, when he invited her to his church, Callie did not sugar coat her answer: "No." He inquired, "Why?" Callie gave him an illustration so that he could get the point of her feelings, "I can get more out of watching the Beverly Hillbillies than going to church."

The Beverly Hillbillies was a comedy television show with people from the mountains who had struck oil and became rich. They moved to the city where they viewed the city people as pretentious and civilization as awkward. Pierre was stunned: "I have never met a southern girl who did not go to church."

Callie came out with, "There is always a first. Here's your first." He said, "If we are going to get married, you have to go to church. Don't you believe in God Callie?" She said, "Of course, I believe in God." Callie went on to tell him that she used to play the piano for the church. He asked, "What happened?"

Reminiscing she said, "I witnessed so much hypocrisy in the church. I asked questions about what I saw, and I was ignored." He seemed to understand; but that did not stop him from continuously inviting her to visit his church. Perseverance on his part paid off, for Callie finally accepted his invitation.

Pierre belonged to a church that had a membership of over five thousand people including many well-known politicians and socialites. Going to church just was not inspiring enough for Callie. Being that she was on a budget, which she watched carefully, she could not believe how often the contribution containers were passed. They passed the collection container at least four times that she could remember for things unrelated to church business. What's more is that she had been accustomed to seeing silver plates passed at the church she attended in Clausell. Imagine this. The size of the container was equivalent to a large aluminum foot tub that a toddler could sit in, but a brown weaved basket that would allow money to be pushed down into it.

She was extremely uncomfortable. For she believed that the attendant who was passing the basket with a type of broom handle, caused the basket to linger right in front of her, forcing her to put something into the basket each time. After the service, Pierre pressed Callie for her thoughts. She shared them: "I heard several young women making fun of the shoes of another young lady that were worn pretty badly. I did not like that. She had two small children and no doubt was struggling financially." Also, Callie mentioned the number of times the collection baskets were passed, as well as, how annoyed she was by that process.

Pierre invited Callie another time to church. Since he had been pressuring her to join, this time Callie thought that she would possibly join his church to appease him. She was prepared mentally to become a member of his church until the minister made a comment that was totally unacceptable to her. With arms spread across the pulpit, multiple diamonds on each of his fingers, the minister said, "We are the Ritz Carlton of all churches." Callie whispered to Pierre, "I am not joining your church today. And furthermore, I am not coming back."

They did not talk about it too much after they got into the car to leave. He accepted her decision not to join his church; however, he was noticeably preoccupied with something else. She asked, "What are you thinking about?" At the beginning, he did not want to tell her. Callie asked, "Are you upset with me because I did not join the church?" He said, "No, it has nothing to do with you." "Callie asked, "Then what is it?"

After continuously nagging him for a response, he said, "I have a bill that I need to pay tomorrow." Callie was thinking about how to make it happen. "I really don't have any extra money either. The little money that I had, I put in the basket at the church." Next, she asked, "How much do you need?" He said, "Five hundred dollars." "What!" She was stumped by his response, as she was thinking seriously about how to help him. She would not dare ask her sister.

162

Also, her close friends were in bad shape financially like Callie.

Then she got an idea; but then, she hesitated because Pierre was a godly man. She started thinking about how others said she looked in her daisy dukes. More than that, how comfortable she felt when she was wearing them.

In the meantime, the question that she had posed when she was left holding all the debt that her ex left her, could now be answered. Would she resist helping a boyfriend for fear that she would get duped again?

Callie was not sure if her earlier catastrophic relationship had been hiding bitterness in the recesses of her heart. Well, she got the answer. Her earlier devastation had not kept her from wanting to help someone that was in need.

About a mile before they reached the exit to where Callie lived, she mustered up courage to share her idea. She said, "I know how you can get the money." He turned to look at Callie. Looking very puzzled, he asked: "How?" Callie said very innocently, "I could win the money." He said, "How?"

Callie said, "I heard on the radio that there was a contest at one of the local night clubs." Pierre rarely went to night clubs because if he had, Callie would have known him. That's probably why Callie assumed that he must have been a little boy when Jason asked her to cook Thanksgiving dinner so that he could bring his *little baby brother* over.

Pierre asked Callie "What kind of contest?" She mumbled, "It's a pretty legs contest." He disappointingly asked, "Are you one of those type of girls?" Callie asked, "What do you mean? You know who I am. What are you asking?" He said, "My best friend and I said that we would never date one of those kinds of girls."

Callie defensively answered, "Whatever you are talking about, that is not me. I was just trying to help you out." Callie shared another fact from her past. "I won a swimsuit competition before." Pierre laughed. That was dangerously offensive to Callie. Perhaps, her demeanor would not allow him to see her as a competitor. Callie said, "Ok, no problem. I was trying to help you. You should know what kind of person that I am. And I strongly resent that you said that. People walk around at the beach with swimsuits on all the time and do people say: 'Oh, are you one of those type of girls?' Just what does that mean?'" She barely inhaled a small breath of air when Pierre interjected: "I am so sorry. So, do you think you can win?" Callie uttered, "Yes."

When they made it to her townhouse, Callie invited her sister to tell Pierre about her previous swimsuit competition. Two of Pierre's old college friends came over for lunch and the entire conversation was about the competition. They had jokes and all Callie could do was let them have their fun. She told them, "It's no big deal. Just skip it."

Anyhow, after they finished lunch, the conversation came up again. Callie showed them the dress that she would wear. It was a red sequence dress with a low-cut v-shaped pattern in the back. The front of the dress was a boat-neck collar, and it was about mid-way her thigh. The dress fit like a glove; but then again, they did not know it because it was on a hanger. Pierre and his friends were determined to see Callie compete.

His friends would not go home, staying from lunch to dinner and until it was time to leave Callie's house. Now, it's time to go the competition and Callie wore a very conservative outfit to the night club. She wore a blue pin-striped suit that was midway her calf.

The time had come for all contestants to register to participate. Callie left her small group of lukewarm supporters to sign up. When she returned, she told the group when the competition was going to start and where the contestants would be found until the competition started.

There were twelve girls taking part. Callie was in the middle of the group. The crowd was huge that night with hardly any room to move around. Callie would wear a red sequence dress that was originally a little below her knee, now it was midway her thigh because she hemmed it for the competition, along with three-inch red Vaneli pumps and a string of pearls. She loved pearls. She would wear a string of pearls with studs or with hoops.

When Callie looked out of the room where the contestants were located, she saw the people leaving the dance floor as the MC quieted the crowd to announce the beginning of the competition. She could not find Pierre along with his curiously nosey naysayer friends. Earlier, each contestant had selected a song to enter the dance floor by either walking or dancing. Callie's turn was about to come up. She put her smile on and walked out. She had a little dance step that was quite simple as she graced the four corners of the dance floor.

There would be no runner-up in the competition. It was all or nothing. The winner would take all. The "all" was five hundred dollars in cash, plus a gift certificate for shoes from one of the local stores. Even though Callie loved shopping for shoes, she wasn't as concerned about the shoes now. An R&B singer would crown the contestant who won.

The winner was named through much anticipation and roars from the audience. So many people were impressed with her grace, style and elegance. The winner was Callie Clausell. The R&B star placed the crown on her head, gave her the five hundred dollars and a bottle of Dom Perignon Champagne. Callie never went backstage again to get the certificate for the shoes, and she left the crown. She took the five hundred dollars, the bottle of champagne and left.

Once Callie received the prize, she walked over to Pierre, handed him an envelope and grinned. "This is for you. You should be able to pay your debt with this." Pierre's brutally honest and suspect friend congratulated Callie, saying: "You know you did not have the prettiest legs; you just had the best charisma and showmanship." Callie agreed with him about her legs, continuing with grace and humility, she said, "Ok, so I got five hundred dollars for having the best showmanship. Any way you look at it, there was only one winner and the winner Callie Clausell, got the money. You Hater."

Pierre told Callie later that he was exceptionally proud of her. He said, "It took a lot of courage to do something like that. I did not realize that you had that type of spunk." Jokingly, Callie could not refuse saying this, "I know you did not realize I had that type of spunk because you thought I was a hoochie momma." She went from a zero to a hero, like wonder-woman in Pierre's time of need in less than eight hours. The laid-back southern girl from Clausell with a nonchalant attitude transformed into a world class competitor which proved to be very valuable. That day, Pierre's view of Callie was bumped up a notch, so much so that he said, "I am indebted to you. I will never forget what you did for me. Never ever. I have never met a person so generous without a hint of an ulterior motive. You gave all your money to me without any hesitation. I know you could have used it."

Her unselfish love was captivating because no doubt she could have used the money. Slowly, Pierre's conversations switched to the kind of wedding that he wanted. Callie told him, "I am not interested in a wedding. I don't have that many close friends. Besides that, I don't think I can afford a big wedding financially or emotionally.

"What do you mean? Most women look forward to a big wedding." She responded, "Most women go into debt with a big wedding. More than that, I do not want to fight with your momma, your grandmomma, or my momma?" "Why would you be fighting?" "Well, my momma is going to want to have the wedding in Clausell. Your momma is going to want to have it in Chicago and your grandmomma is going to want to have it in South Carolina. So, it would be a fight because I want to get married in Atlanta. They were married by a Judge in downtown Atlanta.

There was a glitch right before they got married. Pierre always wanted them to meet to save time because of the distance between where he lived and where Callie lived. Their wedding day was no different. Pierre suggested, "Callie, let's meet at the Civic Center. My roommate works there, and we can all go together to the courthouse. I want him to be our witness." Callie responded, "Ok." She did not think that was too difficult of a request to fulfill.

Callie had just been promoted to a newly created position in a Fortune five hundred company and did not consider taking time off from work. She went to work as usual. If they married on Friday, they would have the weekend for a honeymoon. Callie could come back to work on Monday and later in the year, they could have an extended honeymoon. It sounded like a good plan. Pierre agreed.

When it was time to leave work, Callie mentioned to her co-workers that she was leaving for lunch. As Callie got to the elevator, she returned to say that she might be a little late coming back from lunch because she had something very important to handle. "No problem." said one of the managers. Callie started back to the elevator and thought to herself, "It might take longer than you think. Just say you will be back in a few hours." Callie went back to the same manager and said, "I am so sorry to trouble you. I will be back in a few hours." The manager said, "Is there anything wrong?"

Callie said, "No, I just wanted to cover myself just in case it took longer than normal to finish my business." The manager said, "Are you sure, there is nothing wrong?" Callie came closer to whisper, "Pierre and I are getting married on lunch because I did not want to take time off from work." She said, "What? No way. Just take the rest of the day off."

Callie did not want to drive her car downtown. Consequently, she parked her car at the train station and hopped on a train for downtown. She had never ridden the train before, and she surely did not count on it being a complicated process. It turned out to be difficult for her. When she made it to her stop to get off the train, maybe nerves got in the way because she could not figure out how to get to the building where Pierre and his roommate were waiting.

The train tracks separated the building from easy access. Never did Callie see the stairs that would take her to the building where her future husband was waiting.

After not being able to find the stairs that led to the building, Callie hopped another train to try to back tract. Yet, that did not work either. She exited the station, called her office and the receptionist answered the phone. Callie identified herself and inquired if Pierre had called before the receptionist said, "Pierre has been calling for you for about an hour. Where are you?" Callie said, "I am lost and cannot get to the building." The receptionist said, "He left instructions on how to get to the office. He said you have to find the stairs and that will lead you to the office complex."

Callie tried again, following the instructions Pierre had given the receptionist, only to find that those instructions did not work either. Callie exited the train station again and called her office. The receptionist answered, "Pierre said stay where you are, and he is coming to get you."

Time had flown by so quickly. Callie had not eaten. Her blood sugar plummeted, bringing about uncontrollable jitteriness. It was now almost four p.m., approximately five hours since she had left work at eleven a.m. She exited the train station once again to call her office. The receptionist answered again saying, "Pierre is waiting on you!" Teary-eyed Callie said, "You can tell him. I am not going to marry him. I am going home." At first thought, you might think that Callie took out her frustration on Pierre because she couldn't find her way on the train, a ride which should have taken no more than twenty minutes to get to his roommate's Office building.

The truth of the matter hit Callie hard. What would it have cost Pierre to come pick her up, so they could have gone together? In that case, the so-called saving time cost way more time than what either had hoped would be. Pierre came to her apartment to change her mind about getting married. Callie said, "I am not going to marry you. That's it! It is not meant to be." Pierre apologized for being insensitive about asking Callie to meet him. He said, "I should have come to get you after you could not find the building the first time. If nothing else, I should have been on the side of the train that you exited because it is a complicated entrance for someone not familiar with riding the train. I am deeply sorry." What Callie needed was a good night sleep and maybe she would reconsider.

The following day, Pierre was back trying to get Callie to reconsider her decision. He said, "This time we can go together." So, Monday morning Callie called her office and told the same manager that she did not get married, and she was hesitant to take time off from work again. The manager responded, "The receptionist mentioned your situation to the Vice President of the company, and he asked me to give you the week off with pay. Congratulations!" Callie was overtaken by his generous gift and tearfully replied, "Thank you and please tell him thank you."

Callie and Pierre decided that their wedding attire would be blue pin-striped suits for their big day. When they showed up at the courthouse, the judge that would be officiating asked each of them several questions. He took about fifteen to twenty minutes to talk with them about the length of time they had courted, concluding with, "Do you have a witness?" They said, "No." The judge said, "My assistant will be back shortly, and she can be your witness."

When she returned, they went ahead with the vows. Callie did not have any stress. Additionally, she did not have the stress of paying for a wedding or fighting with family and future in-laws. The only stress Callie had was the previous Friday. They spent four days at the Ritz Carlton for their honeymoon with the assistance of Pierre's cousin who worked there and got the honeymoon suite for them at the employee price.

Callie called Maria first. Callie told her that she and Pierre had just gotten married. Maria said, "April fool." Callie said, "No, I am serious. Pierre and I got married about two p.m. today." Maria again said, "April fool." Callie said, "Momma, this is no April fool joke." Maria said, "You are not going to trick me." Callie was frustrated and said, "Okay, I will call you back in a few days." Callie called Maria again after a few days had passed, repeating what she had told her on April 1st.

Silence came over the telephone. Callie continued after the long silence, "Are you there? Did you hear me momma?" After a long sigh, Maria said, "Well I hope my other girls get married here in Monroeville."

175

Chapter 9: Thought It Was Over

About three months after their wedding, Callie had trouble again. She had sold her house that she bought six years ago. And so now, they lived in the city of about one long block from the bus stop. She had a long exhausting day at work, then a long hard workout at the gym after work. Loaded down with her gym bag, purse and lunch container, she got on the bus about seven p.m. When she reached her stop, she got off the bus and started walking down the hill to their apartment with her gym shoes on for easier walking. There was not a car in sight.

About a half block away from her apartment, a car pulled up beside Callie, and the driver was trying to drive the car onto the sidewalk where she was walking. From the driver's seat, a man flung open the car door on the passenger's side and shouted, "Get in the car!" Callie shouted back, "No!" He shouted again, "Get in the Car!" Callie said, "No!"

The louder he yelled; the louder Callie yelled. She never stopped walking and he was keeping up with her in his car. It seemed like fifteen minutes had passed by, but it was only a few minutes that had elapsed. Suddenly, there was another car turning onto the street, Callie took the opportunity to start running and she crossed over to the other side of the street running and screaming frantically. When she did that, the young male driving the car sped off. Callie did not stop running until she ran upstairs to their neighbor's apartment. The neighbor allowed Callie to sit in his apartment until Pierre came home from work.

When asked by her neighbor what did he look like, she communicated that she only made eye contact with him when he initially yelled at her. She never looked at him after that point, as she continued to say no to his many demands to get into the car. She could not tell you anything else about him or the car except he was a young white male with a lightly bald head and a slim build.

Pierre was sorely troubled by what had occurred. Callie no longer owned a car because she sold it to reduce expenses. She welcomed the opportunity to take public transportation. Her job was one block from the bus stop and everything she needed was on one bus line within a three-mile radius. Keeping expenses down was not a consideration any longer when Pierre considered Callie's safety. He vowed to get another car the following day and he did just that. He did not want her catching the bus at all after that incident.

When they went to pick out a car for Callie, Pierre pointed to a big mustard-yellow car. Although she had a yellow car when she was sixteen years old, that was enough for her. So, she said, "It is a very good price Pierre. Except...no, not that one. It looks like a repainted police car." They finally came across a little car that suited Callie perfectly. He bought it for her.

Pierre knew everything about her financial history. Callie knew everything about his financial history. And they were very conscience about costs and keeping their expenses low. Then, they both relaxed their guard. Callie was confronted with debt again. Between the two of them, they had accumulated sixty thousand dollars' worth of debt after three years of marriage. They both had returned to college, bought two new cars and contemporary furniture. Callie was disappointed in herself. In the worse way, she grumbled to Pierre, "I have worked hard to stay out of debt and here I am again in debt." Callie was not superstitious. Though, she could not ignore the fact that debt had been hanging around her since she couldn't spell it at nine years old.

While Callie knew that Pierre was not going to run away, she blamed herself, even though they both were at fault. Callie felt like a prisoner that had been released from a minor misdemeanor and now went ahead to commit a felony. Debt of sixty thousand dollars was like a felony in comparison to the eleven thousand dollars she was in debt with before.

The young couple filed a Chapter Thirteen. This is when your assets are protected while you are paying off the debt. They repaid the debt in full without ever being late on one payment in five years. That certainly needed mental fortitude, self-control and sacrifices. Callie's felony charge had been reversed. Her creditors did not lose this time and Callie did not feel guilty any longer.

179

During that five-year period while they were under the Chapter Thirteen, Pierre and Callie's friends thought it was exciting that each of them had jobs that required that they travel. Callie traveled on the East Coast, while Pierre traveled on the West Coast. At the beginning, it was fun for them. Each viewed their jobs as an opportunity to learn. Then their feelings changed about their jobs.

Why did their way of thinking change? Callie was responsible for two jobs. Even though she was a traveling facilitator, she had responsibilities as a project coordinator. Pierre's situation was similar. He kept a Junior Level Executive's position, while still in the field as a Sales Consultant. Each only wanted the job they had been in prior to accepting added responsibilities. They expected that they would be compensated after they met the probation period. And yet, it appeared that the probation period would never end. Although, their productivity was noticeable.

Many co-workers assumed that Callie had been demoted. Some asked, "What happened? Why are you not traveling any longer? Did you lose your job? Was it a demotion or a phased-out position?" Callie explained what happened only to those that she felt deserved an answer. To others, she was quiet about it.

Another co-worker felt that Callie was letting women down. Callie responded, "I am not qualified to be the savior for the women of the world." The root of the problem for Callie and Pierre stemmed from the fact that they both were handling responsibilities for two jobs, while only getting paid for one. Monetarily, it did not pay off, and so they re-evaluated the benefits. They decided to stick with just the one job and replace all the extra time geared toward work, to building up their marriage.

Financial calamity also affected family members who through unforeseen events caused debt. Late Sunday afternoon in October 1990, Callie received a call that a terrible accident had occurred. A drunk driver had hit her brother. When she entered the hospital, she went into the intensive care unit to see him. His head was swollen, and his face was unrecognizable. The doctor informed Callie that her brother would not make it through the night. He said, "Gather all of your relatives as soon as possible." Callie and her brother were the only siblings living in Atlanta. Maria, Raoul and the other siblings were living in Monroeville.

Callie felt that Maria would have a nervous breakdown when she heard the news because she was visiting her daddy in Florida who had just experienced a massive stroke. Callie was trying to figure out a way to tell Maria without giving her the doctor's prognosis. She said to Maria, "Raoul, Jr was in a bad car accident, and he is the hospital. Can you come up tonight?" Maria said, "Callie, I will drive up tomorrow." Her momma had never flown before. Again, Callie said, "Momma, a drunk driver hit Raoul Jr.. Please come tonight. Please! I will get a flight for you." Maria maintained her position, "Callie, I will be up tomorrow because I want to spend one more night with my daddy."

Callie knew Maria would not forgive her if Raoul Jr. had died without her getting a chance to see him. Callie was left with no other choice but to explain the reason for the urgency. "The Doctor said he will not make it through the night." As soon as Callie said that Maria had a loud eruption, "Oh, no God! Oh, no! Not my son! Please! Not my son." Her piercing scream caused Maria's step-momma to take the phone and ask, "What did you tell your Momma?" Callie repeated what she said to Maria. Maria's step-momma reprimanded Callie. "You should not have done that." Callie did not care about her reprimand because she had done the right thing by her momma. Maria would have never forgiven Callie if she had not shared with her the urgency of coming to Atlanta.

Callie made the flight arrangement, and it would be Maria's first flight ever to make, as well as make it alone. When Maria hit Atlanta, her daughter and son-in-law picked her up from the airport. When they made it to the hospital, Raoul Jr. was in a coma in intensive care. His head was swollen so large that his face was distorted. His eyes looked as if he had been continuously hit in them. Cuts and bruises were all over his body. His wife and children were crying nonstop. When the doctor entered, he gave them the news again. It was a death sentence. He would not make it through the night.

Raoul Jr. lived through the night. The doctor could not believe it. Days went by and weeks went by. Eventually, he came out of the coma. He was unable to speak, and he stared at everyone with his glassy looking eyes. Family members from all over the southeastern United States were visiting Raoul Jr. They did not have much to say other than just stare back at him.

The emotional and financial drain was enormous on the family who traveled back and forth to the hospital regularly. Yet, Raoul Jr. was never left alone. While on their shift with him, after Callie and Pierre had prepared their cots for sleep and had gotten all bedded down, they heard him say, "Mah-Mah."

Those words were his first since his car accident, almost three months later. Immediately, they called Maria to tell her. When the doctor came the following day for his visit, he was enthusiastic about the breakthrough. He told the family that Raoul Jr. would have a long journey ahead of himself. And each member of the family would play a vital role in his recovery, beginning with recreating his memory because of the extensive brain damage. The family rose to the challenge and even included his three-year-old daughter in his rehabilitation process.

The change in Raoul Jr.'s financial circumstances caused his oldest child to act out. From the start, Raoul Jr. was too liberal with giving his ten-year-old son so much money. When his daddy was not able to give it, the son changed, becoming more aggressive.

Although the family got some of the best assistance for brain injured patients, the financial hardship was still at the forefront of Raoul Jr's family and all the other family members. Because everyone was so exhausted, tempers flared with terrible accusations against one another. "I am doing more than you. You are not doing what you are supposed to do."

That was unfortunate. They were all completely involved in his recovery in one way or another. Consequently, bickering should not have existed. Giving help should not have been a competition between them. Reasoning on the point that anything you can contribute is worthwhile and that there are so many ways to render aid was the way to approach the situation, although everyone has limitations.

Love, not conflict, should have been the dominating force. Learning that only committing to what you can afford financially is one form of protection from debt. Only committing to what you can afford mentally or emotionally protects your soundness of mind. That was the balanced view for each to take. Reasonableness was not happening.

During Raoul Jr.'s hospitalization, additional financial hardship hit Callie and Maria hard. They had not eaten at all during the day. They stopped by a restaurant near the hospital to get a sandwich. They devoured the sandwich because Maria needed to get to the hospital to relieve another family member. Callie dropped Maria at the hospital for her shift and left for home.

Sometime later Callie began to feel sick. She was hot one minute and cold the next, taking off her clothes, then putting them back on. Later, her stomach began swelling to the point that her waistline's measurement went from twenty-five inches to the equivalency of a woman five to six months pregnant. Her stomach looked like a basketball was in it. Callie threw up until she could not throw up anymore. She was crawling on the floor to reach the cool tile in the bathroom which was soothing to her face. She slept in that position all night long on the bathroom floor.

She heard the phone ring. She was unable to move. Through all of that, Pierre never woke up, never went to the bathroom. When he got up the next morning to take his shower, he found Callie asleep on the bathroom floor. "What happened? Callie, get up. Get in the bed." While trying to get Callie off the floor, Callie slurred, "I am sick. Please call my job and notify them that I will not be coming in today because I am sick." She walked two feet to the master bedroom and lay down on the floor, where she stayed all day asleep.

Callie knew Pierre had an eight-a.m. meeting that he could not miss. He got his briefcase and yelled from the other room, "I will be in an all-day meeting. Please get some rest today. I will check with you later." Out the door he went. She lay on the floor with the telephone beside her when she mustered up enough energy to check the voicemail. It was Maria who had called. She had been admitted into the hospitable. Subsequently, they treated her intravenously for food poisoning. In her voicemail, she wanted Callie to come down and care for her brother. Of course, Callie could not make it, nor did she have the energy to telephone Maria as she placed the phone on the floor beside her. Her intention was to go back to the bathroom because the floor was cool. She did not make it back there either.

About four p.m. her telephone rang, and she woke up. She managed to pick up the receiver. It was a friend who had called Callie at work, only to find out she was at home sick. By then Callie was intensely ill. When she answered the telephone, she recognized it was her friend. Callie asked in a very weak voice, "Please call Pierre to let him know I am going to go to the emergency room and to please meet me there." Callie threw on a dress and headed to the emergency clinic, barely making it there when she staggered in and almost fell from dehydration. She received the same diagnosis as her momma, a severe case of food poisoning.

Callie could not go to work for three weeks because of the food poisoning. Besides that, she was unable to take her shift with her brother, so most of her shift fell upon Maria.

When Callie returned to work, her manager's boss asked how she was doing. She told him she was better, but she was still experiencing nausea. He told Callie he had been food poisoned before and was sick for a few days. Callie asked, "Did you sue the restaurant for damages? He replied, "No, it was not worth it." Callie said, "I am going to sue for damages." He tried to discourage her by saying, "You will not get anything because you will have to prove that you were food poisoned at their restaurant and not something you prepared. That's difficult to prove.

Furthermore, if you get a lawyer and you win the case, you will have to pay the lawyer's fee. That would dip into your compensation. Your insurance will pay for medical costs. Your sick leave will cover your days absent. So, it is not worth it." Callie questioned him, "What about pain and suffering? He said, "Why bother? It will just tie you up. Besides, I know a friend that was food poisoned and he was sick for about as long as you were. He sued and never received compensation.

Callie quickly said, "Then your friend must not have been as sick as I was." Callie was confident that she would be compensated.

She asked Pierre to visit the restaurant to tell them of her illness related to food poisoning that she had gotten from eating there. The owner of the restaurant suggested that Callie follow up with the restaurant's insurance company. She wrote a letter to the contact he gave Pierre at the insurance company. She included receipts and asked for pain and suffering. An adjuster from the restaurant's insurance company called Callie after two months saying that they wanted to settle with her.

The insurance adjuster felt that the offer was generous. Not to tie up any more time, Callie accepted the offer. The check was written to Callie and her husband, and it went on to say on the pay-to line: Her Name, Her Husband's Name, As Husband and Wife and Individually. Callie received five thousand dollars. Unfortunately, Maria did not file a claim. However, Callie split the money with her momma, fifty-fifty. Callie knew that her momma deserved much more money because she suffered from severe colitis. The bottom line was Maria was still overcome with her son's health and Callie did not have time to pursue it. A monetary loss for Maria.

Callie asked an older retired attorney friend, "Why did the insurance company write the check with my name, my husband's name, as husband and wife and as individuals?" He said, "So that Pierre could not come back and file an independent claim." He went on to say, "Pierre could ask for pain and suffering, and he could possibly get money for the time that he missed from work, caring for you. Since he is in sales, the insurance company would have to pay him money based upon what a sales rep makes in his industry. They have to pay on potential sales he could have made."

Callie learned something new. To say the least, her boss and his boss were surprised when Callie disclosed to them both that she received a settlement of five thousand dollars.

Raoul Jr.'s family was in chaos. Many rallied together and paid some car payments and other important bills. The rest of them did what they could to assist financially, though small in comparison to what was needed. Within two years he was reduced to below poverty level. He lost everything. He and his wife separated, and she moved in with his best friend, having several children for him. The best friend took care of all her financial needs. The nephew started having serious problems. He went to jail for selling drugs to get money and by now the daughter started acting out. All because of this one word, debt. All the hard work and financial security Raoul Jr. had built for his family was gone after one car accident. Callie saw that any unexpected incidents can cause debt, whether financial, emotional, or moral. Like Callie, debt became one of Raoul's enemies.

To change her focus concerning money and debt, Callie wanted to do something that would make her life have more meaning. Now, she and Pierre had no debt, so she left her job and started her volunteer work in September 1993. In November 1993, they moved from their apartment and leased a commercial building for her husband's business. It was going to be a live/workspace.

Callie felt this would be a terrific opportunity to set up a loft apartment. It was about eighteen hundred square feet. She sectioned the room into an office space, living room, dining room, and bedroom within the one large room. In the second room, she used it for their kitchen and storage of their inventory. She bought a two-eyed stovetop and mini refrigerator. She moved their furniture in and voila, a beautiful, yet extremely functional combination living and working area.

Then Callie walked into the small room near the wall of power meters. When she opened the door to the small room which was the bathroom, there was only a toilet and a rusty basin. There was no shower stall or tub. She had forgotten about the condition of the bathroom. Earlier on, Callie was thrilled about the opportunity to combine the two spaces. Now she was confronted with overcoming doubt.

Was it possible for her to install a shower or tub? No, because they had limited funds. At that moment, she had to use the bathroom. She was too afraid to close the door. Therefore, she left it open. She looked up into the ceiling of the bathroom while in her seated position. A disturbing image met her eyes. Junk was falling out of the ceiling, like dirty foam and cotton and spider webs, which she hated all three.

Callie's memory defaulted to the time she saw the soiled cotton with dirty foam bursting from the sofa's arm and seat of her grandmomma's friend. Callie did not want to sit down on that sofa. It gave her the "heebee geebees" as they used to say. The ceiling had now given Callie the "heebee geebees." She tried to turn on the squeaky water faucet to wash her hands. The pressure of the water was so low she could not stay any longer. So, she did a fast walk from the bathroom.

Shortly thereafter, she spoke to her husband about her problem. She mentioned that she could not go into the bathroom. She said, "The foam hanging from the ceiling gave me the creeps." Do you know what he said? He said, "Just don't look up." Callie was livid!

She now had to find a better solution. Her solution was within fifty feet. When Callie had to use the bathroom, she would go to a restaurant across the street. Well that solved one problem. One down and one to go. How would they take showers? Until something else became available, they would have to use the rusty basin. Incredible! Within the week, they had been given a free year's membership to a health club about two blocks away.

They had been prior members but had cancelled their membership because it became unaffordable. They were informed that they had won a free year because all their referrals had joined the club. Callie and Pierre did not know that the program existed. Can you believe it? Another solution to a major problem for Callie. She was feeling pretty good. You may wonder how that was a solution to a problem. Not just a solution, but an upgraded solution!

Well, the gym had showers available, steam room, hot tub, fresh towels and a food bar.

They went to the gym twice per day. Many at the gym thought that they were serious about working out, although they were gaining weight. They were considered gym rats. Also, club members as well as employees began to ask questions like, "What did you do today." Callie would laugh and say, "Nothing much. Just took a shower." Another day while in the locker room, an acquaintance asked, "Were you in the class just now? Callie said, "No, I took a shower and just relaxed." They did not have the presence of mind to work out. That went on for six months. Since they were young, they could endure. They were confident that eventually the business would take off and they would do well.

The first sale that her husband made was eight dollars and sixty-three cents. Callie knew not to laugh. She said, "Congratulations! Wow, your first check in the basement." That is what they called their warehouse because of the underground location.

No creditors were calling them. They were making it. But, they had no extra money. They had a little hiccup with the bathroom. But so far, they stayed positive until they got their first electric bill of over six hundred dollars. How in the world could they afford that? The building that they leased was in a strip mall where longtime businesses were located, a furniture store, a jewelry store, a shoe store and a clothing store.

The entrance was in the back of the building below the shoe store on the corner underground. On a five-year lease, they received the first year free which was a sweet deal because it would allow them some time to get their business up and running. The meter for electric usage for all the businesses was in their warehouse that they interchangeably referred to as the basement.

It just so happened, a representative from the power company came to read the meter. Callie was in the bed asleep. He scared her to death when he walked in. As she was opening her eyes, she yelled, "Who is it?" She knew that it could not be Pierre. He always let Callie know by knocking on the door, then saying her name before entering.

When her eyes were fully opened, Callie saw a man in a uniform. He saw her at the same time she saw him. He stopped and said, "I didn't know anyone lived here." She pulled the covers up while sitting up in the bed and said, "Yes, we moved into the space one month ago. We live here and work here. What are you doing in here?" He explained, "I came to read the meter."

He did not seem to be a threat. Still, Callie was afraid. She tried to keep her composure as she crawled out of bed. She said, "Well anyway, I am glad you are here. I keep the lights turned off unless I need the light. I don't keep the air conditioner running all the time and my power bill is so expensive. Can you help me?"

He was very pleasant. He said, "The reason that the power bill is costly is because it is zoned for commercial use." Callie asked, "Can we get it zoned for residential use?" He gave Callie instructions on what to do. Next, he said he would follow up with the power company by confirming that they were indeed living there.

He did as he said he would do because when she followed up with the power company, the customer service rep said a note had been placed in the account concerning the living situation. They could have their space rezoned to residential use by the power company. For sure, their bills dropped dramatically. The company reduced the bill of six hundred dollars to a little over twenty-five dollars.

Keeping their food costs low could be a plus for the new business owners if they had a kitchen. The modest two-eyed hot plate was enough. Since their lifestyle was simple, it allowed them to move forward. You have heard the saying, "Attitude is everything." Attitude was everything in their situation, which helped them to still be positive.

Following the first six months of only taking a shower at the gym, Callie and Pierre began to get their exercise routine pumped up by running. Because they were feeling energized, their sales increased. When Pierre reviewed their income and expenses, he decided that they had enough money to lease a condo.

Although their expenses had decreased in several areas, their food costs had increased. In the meantime, the well-known jeweler in the small center needed more space. The young couple sublet the space to the jeweler for the remaining part of the five-year lease without any problems. Subletting the space was a great business move.

Chapter 10: Calm Then the Storm

For two years, their life was stable. Things were calmer than usual, relatively speaking. Although they owned a commissioned-based business, their income was steady. Their condo lease was about to end. This prompted them to ask the owner if he were interested in selling. They received an astounding yes.

Given that two challenges existed, they really needed to think this all the way through. The first challenge involved getting qualified for a loan. The second challenge was where would they park their delivery truck. They had recently learned that it violated the by-laws of the association.

Sometime during their lease, they had their company's name placed on the van. It was terrific advertising for them. But they overlooked a crucial element that was highlighted under the by-laws of the association. Commercial vehicles were not allowed to park on the premises overnight. Pierre and Callie had assumed that it did not apply to residents.

After they were informed by the association about the specifics of the rule, they had to leave their van in the mall parking lot close to where they lived. The basement was no longer available to store inventory. Most of the inventory was kept on the truck. Parking during the day was no problem, just the nighttime parking. If someone stole the truck while it was parked in a nearby shopping mall, they would be out of business pronto.

The owner of the property now started to put pressure on them because he wanted to sell quickly. It was obvious that they were making money based upon their bank statements. They started the loan process by completing the application along with giving the required documents. To the point of securing a loan, more was needed than making money. You had to have a good credit score. After that extensive process, the banker said that the bank would not extend the loan. "In a year," she said. "This will give you the opportunity to clean up a few minor things on your credit.

The owner of the property had given them two weeks to put a contract on the condo. As that did not happen; once again, Pierre and Callie had to move. Where would they live? There was no time to find an affordable place that would meet their upgraded standards. They moved into a low-end motel far from their center of business activity and friends.

When you are younger, some of the things that you may have considered exciting can become scary when you are older. Callie was there. Here they were again, trying to figure out what to do. This time no debt, just embarrassed. Having a place to live was a basic part of life. To that extent, they were having difficulty fulfilling that basic need. Consistently, Callie said, "We are business owners. We appear to be intelligent. Why can't we figure this out? What are we missing?"

After staying in this low-end motel for three months, Callie spoke candidly to Pierre: "I don't want to move again until I get a house." After her first house which she bought at nineteen years old, she had never wanted to buy another house. She liked having close neighbors. Apartment and condo living were what she enjoyed. Truth be told, all the moving around was now beginning to affect her. She wanted something that a few years earlier did not matter to her. Callie wanted a permanent address. Callie wanted a house.

She felt getting a house with a big garage would solve several problems, namely, protection of their inventory, provide office space and living accommodation. In their quest to expand, Callie and Pierre had already hired a secretary, and a couple of sales consultants, who worked on a draw against commission. It seemed like a big house would do the job if they had excellent credit.

They would have to come up with money without support from a bank or personal investor. They were switching money around alternating between paying personal bills one month and the next month paying business bills.

Pierre tried his best to work it out to please Callie. He went on the hunt for a house. He found a house for lease with the option to buy for three hundred and fifty thousand dollars. He told Callie it had a huge garage, big enough to park an Econoline van in it and her new Volvo. Yes, Pierre surprised Callie with a new Volvo.

She was nervous when he took her to look at the empty house. It was about nine p.m. They sat outside in the car by the mailbox. The lights were on. They viewed the stunning chandelier, which gave the house an overall look of elegance. The house had a cathedral ceiling throughout. The best feature was that it would be great for entertaining.

The open floor plan flowed easily from room to room, very open and airy. It was five thousand square feet. That was more than enough living space for two people and a small business. The address was catchy to Callie: One Regal Trace. Callie remembered saying to Pierre, "Do you think God is going to let us have this house?" He said, "Yes! I have absolute confidence." They were extremely motivated when they drove away. The next day Pierre contacted the realtor who worked out the details concerning the lease purchase. Sure enough, they bought the house the following year. The month that they closed on the house, the hot water heater exploded, and it was one problem after another.

Callie learned that it can be very easy to get into a house. Maintaining occupancy was the challenge. Just because you are paying rent at one thousand dollars per month, does not mean you can afford a house at the same rate. Unlike most apartment complexes who take care of repairs, the homeowner handles repairs, yard maintenance, utilities, taxes, mortgage, insurance and if the house is in a gated community, Home Owners' Association (HOA) fees for other amenities.

One of Callie's friend's felt that she could own a house for the money she paid for rent. As she and Callie were riding through a neighborhood, Callie pointed out the leaves on the roof, which appeared to have been there for a while. The grass was not cut. The yard was not manicured. The house needed painting. Callie asked her, "How will you handle all of those expenses with only a one-thousand-dollar budget for housing, especially in the neighborhood that you are wanting to move?" Additionally, she asked, "What if the roof leaks or the hot water heater goes out?" Her friend got the point.

Emotionally, she equated buying a house with having a home. "An apartment can be a home." Callie informed her. "And purchasing a house does not make it a home." Callie told her friend to check with her apartment manager to get permission to paint the apartment, hang pictures and wallpaper. Overall, she encouraged her to treat her apartment like she would treat the house she had wanted to purchase. "Make it yours."

She did, and it looked great. Each room had a personality. Her friend liked the results and most importantly, she avoided the heartache of buying something she could not avoid at that time. Callie wished she had gotten that type of advice as a reminder. Well, she was happy for her friend and proud of her for listening, since from time-to-time Callie's advice or decisions were not on point. Callie knew though that often people will not listen to you if they feel you are not prosperous, or you have made multiple mistakes. In this case, her friend listened, and she escaped a potential trap.

A good part of the money from the first-year lease was used for the couple's down payment on the house the following year. The banker who had previously rejected their loan for the condo had now become an independent mortgage broker. She called the couple to let them know she was now in her own business and could help them with the purchase of a house if they were still interested.

The couple had a tax liability that they needed to clear up; so, she referred a tax accountant to them. The mortgage broker said that the person who she was referring had great credentials. He had helped people with serious tax problems and that he was a former employee of the Internal Revenue Service (IRS). She assured Callie and Pierre that he would be the one to help them.

Callie had no other questions since the mortgage broker was thorough in her explanation of how to cut the liability, as well as her recommendation of the professional tax accountant. Elated by the potential help they would receive, Callie gave the credit of her help to God, thinking, "Wow, she is really going to help us. This is a blessing from God." Not true. God's blessings are without pain. And their pain with this person was increasing.

Over the years, they had consistently looked for an experienced and affordable tax accountant to come up with a good tax plan for them. Referrals from others did not always work out. They knew it was essential to have a tax accountant to give professional counseling. Then they acted on that basic knowledge, hiring different accountants to help them with their desire to have a strong tax plan.

Callie kept all their yearly tax returns; although, this year would be slightly different. There were multiple tax returns that the referred tax accountant sent to the IRS. This is what was revealed. While Callie was looking at the tax return more closely, for whatever reason, she discovered an error, which was significant. She spoke to the broker about the tax accountant she had referred. The broker wrote down that she would talk with him.

Callie was not satisfied that he had not followed up with her. She found a number for him and called him. When Callie asked to speak with him, the receptionist said, "I don't think he is in today." Callie asked a few more questions and could verify that he worked part time at JC Penny as a janitor! Callie left a message for him again and he did not return her call on that occasion.

Pierre and Callie thought that he worked for an accounting firm, and he had a home office. They came to that conclusion based upon his business card. They were not thorough in getting more information on his credentials. The tax returns that he prepared showed that they had made more money than she thought. The truth of the matter was they were not sure how much money they had made exactly, just a good guess from the bank statements.

Not having that information prepared, made it easier for the tax accountant to guess on the higher end. An income tax return preparer is quite different from a Certified Public Accountant (CPA). Callie and Pierre really needed a CPA. Foremost, was that they needed guidance and recommendations for a good tax plan. After that was achieved, they wanted that person to prepare all their tax returns.

To fix the error Callie had brought to his attention, required that he prepare another return. More errors surfaced, then another return had to be prepared and then another return. They were so deep in the process that they ignored the fact that he was not qualified; and they were not prepared to continue.

209

The point is that they ignored the obvious because of two body parts: their eyes and their heart. The insatiable eye took over. They saw the house and they wanted it. Callie had read in the Bible that a person's heart can betray him. Who can know it? That now applied to them. Surely, it did.

After a while, the tax preparer called them to come to his home office to sign another amended tax return. When they went to his office, Callie voiced her concerns about the errors and many amended tax returns. He apologized for the errors and omissions and agreed that he would refund their money. He lied about that as well as he never mailed all of the amended tax returns. Guess how many red flags that raised to the Internal Revenue Service?

The couple just made all kinds of mistakes, and the mistakes were gaining momentum. Callie and Pierre were stabbing themselves all over. They just should have walked away from the deal. The banker, turned mortgage broker, had now fulfilled her role as intermediary for the loan. Her fee was thirteen thousand dollars for that service. Then there was the realtor's commission. And all of that was financed. Although their mortgage was unbelievably high, they were making the payments. Another false sense of security was thinking that everything was working out and they were doing well. It was all an illusion.

For one reason or another, they had friends that were always giving them commendation. That could have contributed to their hesitancy to walk away from the house deal or the fear of friends. They had a fear of embarrassment if their friends saw them walk away from such a beautiful home. During that time, they won distributor of the year from one of the manufacturers that they represented. The prize was two roundtrip tickets to St. Lucia with hotel accommodations for seven days to one of the best resorts in the world.

Following their return from St. Lucia, it was no different. Many of Callie and Pierre's friends said that the couple had made a strong impact on them. It appeared that they were prospering, and their friends were encouraged by that part. That false sense of security was dominant. Nevertheless, something changed drastically.

Chapter 11: What Would They Do?

Pierre and Callie were distributors for several product lines. Only one of the contracts they held was their main source of income. Without notice or consideration of the fact that the young couple had pioneered this product line, the company ended the contract. "What happened?" Callie asked her husband.

He said, "The President of the company felt that we breached the contract." Callie asked, "How so?" Pierre said, "The President said that we had signed a no compete agreement and we breached it when we represented another company at the trade show." Pierre assured Callie that he never would have done that. Their next course of action was to review the files.

On one hand, Callie felt that they had not signed the agreement. On the other hand, she felt that we all make mistakes and she had signed something without paying attention. Her ability to organize data, keep important documents and whatever it took to keep the office running smoothly was her strength. The contract was in the file. The no compete page of the contract was not in the file. Callie gasped for breath. Tears welled up in her eyes. She felt that she had done something wrong.

Destructive thinking appeared as it had done in the past, even if there were no concrete evidence. The feeling of failure was like someone who had a choke hold on her, and she could not breathe. It would not go away. Could Callie have taken a more positive view? Thinking in this way would have been better. "I file all important documents, especially those with our signatures on it. If this page of the contract is missing, there is a reason for it, we did not sign it." She chose to think negative, not positive. You can imagine why with her history.

Soon they were put at ease. You will never guess what took place. The secretary to the President of the product line which was their main source of income called. She said,

"Mr. Monk asked me to pull the copy of your signed no compete agreement for his review. I only have the blank copy in my file. Could you please forward a copy of your signed agreement for my records?" She wanted to know if they could fax a copy of the signed document to her. Was she joking? Was she inquisitive as to why he wanted that document?

One way you can look at this situation is that the President did not share the reason why he needed it; because if he had, it would have been clear to her that she should not have asked us for a copy. Anyway, she made the young couple happy.

It would not have been a big thing for the secretary to ask Callie for a document that Pierre or she had signed, given that they had a good working relationship. The secretary knew that they had been ethical in their distribution of the product line, never diverting the product or compromising the standard set. Unknowingly, she proved that a signed copy of the no compete agreement did not exist.

Why then did the President send a letter saying that they had indeed signed a no compete agreement as a reason for ending their contract? What an embarrassing assumption! Could there have been another motive for canceling the contract instead of what was given? Where was the manufacturer's loyalty to his number one distributor?

No doubt, he had required that all his distributors sign a no compete agreement. When Pierre became his first distributor, the manufacturer had not advanced to that stage in his business. The product line was only yielding about eight hundred dollars per month in the marketplace according to the company's records. So that explains why they had not signed that addendum to the first contract. It was not in force at that time. It would make sense that as the company grew, they may have required that a no compete agreement be signed by the prospective distributors annually.

According to Callie's husband, signing that addendum to the contract would have made them a single line distributor. In that case, that would not have been good for them financially because they carried other product lines prior to entering into a contractual agreement with this company. If the manufacturer did not agree with Pierre's refusal to sign a no compete clause, why did the manufacturer renew the contract? Why did the company end the contract six months into the agreement after several years of distribution?

Interestingly, the same company that had abruptly ended their contract without any discussion or notice, awarded them the trip to St. Lucia for exceeding their sales goals for the year, in addition to achieving their sales goals for the past two years. Since the manufacturer was gaining market share steadily, the company was trying to convert their distributors to employees, working directly for the company as a manufacturer's representative. Pierre had been approached about working as a manufacturer's rep. His salary would have been set and the earning potential would have been limited.

With that advance knowledge, Pierre felt that the company would find another way around removing them from the picture after he had declined the offer. It really did not matter to this company that they had not signed a no compete clause. The wheels of injustice were moving forward.

The plot thickens. Notice the sequence of events that caused the manufacturer to state that they had indeed signed a no compete clause. First, one of the biggest trade shows was in the summer. During this show, distributors sell their products to a group of over one hundred thousand attendees. This is the opportunity to get ahead financially for manufacturers, distributors and the individual sales consultants. In one weekend, many of their sales consultants could pay off small debts and get ahead. That's how important it was to take part in this trade show.

Pierre had inquired about the manufacturer's participation in the show. The response was, "We are not going to participate this year." Pierre was disappointed. He explained the predicament that the President's decision would put him and his sales team in financially. None of them would make the money that they were depending on from that show. The manufacturer did not care because the company was gaining market share and so his decision was final, but not to Pierre.

Previously, Pierre and Callie had taken part in that same show with one of the other product lines that they had a contract to distribute. That product line did not do as well at this actual show. Thus, it would not have done well again and so with that information, Callie's husband started searching for manufacturers to represent at the show. He found one and informed the President that since the company would not be participating in the show, the couple and their team would be representing another manufacturer. In all fairness, Pierre gave him a grand opportunity to be compassionate and do the right thing.

Whether the company thought Pierre was bluffing or not, they did not respond. Nevertheless, they found out later that the company Pierre and Callie were going to represent at the show and the company that they were under contract with were not just competitors, the men in charge hated each other. It was now clear that the no compete clause that they did not sign, did not matter. The husband-and-wife team were caught in the middle. A war was about to start.

It was hardly the time to turn over and die. Callie and Pierre had worked too hard to get their company to this level. They were making their sales goals as outlined by the manufacturer. The manufacturer was just trying to strong-arm this little fledgling company. One of Callie's dear friends knew of the situation. He had a good sense of humor, encouraging them to keep their chins up. He made this comment, "You are not in business until you get a good lawsuit." They hired a very competent attorney to fight their battle. Immediately though, there were a couple of challenges.

The obvious challenge was the couple were owners of a small company that could not continuously dish out the bucks without consequences. The second trial occurred in the middle of the battle. Pierre and Callie's attorney was diagnosed with breast cancer. She could not continue to represent them; and so, they had to find new representation. Being completely dumbfounded about the whole succession of events, Callie asked, "Is this for real?"

Yes, it was for real and in the meantime, they started

to feel the hurt financially. Slowly, they were going into debt. They put their house up for sale. Many potential buyers came to view the house, but no interest. Their house was on the market for about a year. Their money was almost depleted.

Callie and Pierre were concerned about their staff, which included how they would pay them. They found jobs for as many of the staff as they could. They were confronted with losing everything they had worked so hard to achieve. To handle the stress, the couple started running six miles four times per week to reduce stress. They had run about three blocks from their house when Callie staggered and fell to the ground. She struggled to get up but could not. When she was finally able to stand up with Pierre's help, Callie knew instantly that something was terribly wrong with her body.

She went to her doctor where her preliminary diagnosis was possibly appendicitis. To be sure, the doctor suggested that Callie have a procedure that would allow the doctor to view Callie's entire abdominal cavity. Callie hesitated at first because she had never had surgery. Within a few weeks, she reconsidered and had the procedure performed.

Her doctor was a very calm person with a very soothing Southern voice. While in her office on her first visit, she calmly said, "Callie, the location of the pain could also indicate that there is something wrong with one or more of your reproductive organs." They went through this tiresome dialogue.

The doctor asked, "Callie, what if it is not your appendix and it's your ovary? What would you like me to do?" Callie responded, "Please fix it or remove it." Next, she said, "Callie, what if it is not your ovary? What if it is your fallopian tube? What would you like me to do?" Callie said, "Look Doctor Serenade, you only have one chance to go into my abdomen. I have never had surgery; therefore, whatever needs repairing or removing, please do so before you exit."

Pierre supported Callie's decision and Callie trusted that Doctor Serenade would do the right thing and she did. She had taken photographs of Callie's abdominal cavity. Her liver, appendix, ovaries, fallopian tubes were fine. Covering

221

her ovaries and parts of her intestine were little brown threads of tissue that had traveled to those locations and settled. The diagnosis was endometriosis.

Endometriosis was what had caused Callie's severe pain. The disease had traveled to her ovaries, bladder, and intestine. In severe cases, it could travel to other organs such as the liver. Since this tissue was in a place that was uncommon, it could not leave the body. Surgery was needed to clean up the misplaced tissue.

Callie's doctor told her that in some cases the disease returns. Callie asked the doctor how she could prevent it from coming back. She said, "Sometimes having a baby helps." Callie said, "Okay, let me see if I understand. Let's say I have a baby. Could it return after the baby is born?" She said, "Possibly." Callie said, "That would not be wise to have a baby now with the hope that it would not return. That is not an option for me. I will take my chances. No baby." Very often, they had very candid talk. They just moved right along to the next conversation. The disease did not come back. Callie was fortunate since she read about many women who were diagnosed with endometriosis who were experiencing the symptoms within three months of surgery. Callie was happy that she and Pierre had medical insurance. Without that, she would not have been able to have the procedure.

Not long after that, Callie was hit with another one of the woes of life, death. Her favorite relative, Granddaddy Louie, who was mentioned earlier, died. She was losing her home, her business, her health, and now her granddaddy Louie had died. This was all in the same year. What more could happen? Callie felt like the Bible Character Job. He lost his cattle, flocks, and his ten children all in one day. After that he was afflicted with a disgusting, painful disease. He had friends that thought he was doing something wrong to incur God's anger. But that was not true. What more could happen to him? His wife told him to curse God and die. Callie knew better than to do that!

Chapter 12: Was It Really Light?

Perhaps you have heard this saying, "There is light at the end of the tunnel." Well the devastated duo had an unbelievable opportunity to save their home and rebuild their business. Callie asked Pierre, "Where is this opportunity?" He said, "We have to fly to Dubai."

Callie stared at him and timidly replied, "Dubai? I am not going to Dubai. Isn't all the fighting in the Middle East near Dubai?" Pierre said, "It's in another part of the Middle East." In the same timid manner, Callie asked, "Are you crazy Pierre? Has our situation caused you to put your life on the line? As far as I am concerned, you can take your best friend with you and if he cannot go, you have my permission to take your momma along."

"Callie, it is a grand opportunity, a very rich country and we can visit our friends in London on the way back." "Is that supposed to make me forget about how I feel?" Pierre was thrilled and went hurrying off to share that information with all who would listen.

Well, it turned out that Pierre could not travel without Callie. "We are a package deal" so he said. Reluctantly, Callie agreed to go, even though Pierre was oblivious to Callie's traumatic feeling. Pierre was eager about the opportunity to work and nothing else appeared to matter.

Although the flight was eighteen hours long, flying first class made it easier. They flew from Atlanta to London nonstop and from London to Dubai nonstop. The flight to Dubai was extremely comfortable. Each passenger had a separate seat that turned, rocked and reclined. The free mini bottles of Scotch helped calm Callie's nerves because she drank her bottle and sometimes Pierre's bottle when the flight attendant came by. After then, they could have gone to the moon and Callie would not have cared. The company who sponsored their trip had a car waiting for them when they arrived at the airport in Dubai.

The driver took them to their hotel, where they had a visitor waiting for them. It was the sister of Callie's friend who had been living in Dubai for some years. That was comforting to see a familiar face. After their brief visit with her, she left, and they went to sleep. The next morning when the couple went to the office, to Callie's surprise, it was just like offices in the United States.

While driving to the office, Callie saw a Rolls Royce, then another and for a while that is mostly what she saw or fixed her eyes upon. She told Pierre, "I have seen as many Rolls Royce automobiles here as I have seen Ford automobiles in the United States."

Between watching the news and reading the newspaper, they discovered that it was much like the United States in several areas. In many areas, it was different. For one thing, they were told that there was no unemployment. They felt that the statement could not be right. They were also told that the crime rate was zero, nonexistent. Okay, they thought about that and remembered what her friend told her what was the penalty for returning a check. If it were because of insufficient funds, one would serve three years in jail. Of course, that would deter crime. Still, they couldn't believe there was no crime. In any case, Callie wanted to get to the business, finish it as quickly as possible and return to Atlanta.

Pierre asked Callie, "Would you like to check out the city? Take a walk or jog?" Callie thought that he was not well. She asked, "Are you feeling okay?" "Me?" "Yes, you." Pierre answered, "I feel pretty good. That is why I thought you might have wanted to go. How are you feeling?" Callie said, "Oh Pierre, I must be delusional. I thought you asked me to go for a jog. I guess I did not hear that." Pierre confirmed, "Yes, that is what I asked." Callie said, "Oh, then you definitely must not feel well, and you should not go. There is no way I'm going anywhere without a driver." Pierre smiled and said, "I'll see you later."

Instead of walking or jogging around the city, Callie locked the door, put a do not disturb sign on the door and decided to watch television. She could not believe that she found a Hip-hop dance show with dance moves and music like the music in the United States. The only thing was that she just could not understand what they were singing because it was in a foreign language. What do you know? That was the same with some music in the United States.

227

Callie could not understand the lyrics even though it was in English.

Their sole purpose for being in Dubai was to conduct a test of the products that they were to distribute in the United States. Pierre and Callie, along with the investor's representatives prepared a salon near the hotel to conduct the test. The representative for the investor mentioned that it was very difficult to find African models with the different hair types and textures. In fact, he was grim about it. Little did they know that the sister of Callie's friend knew of a hair salon quite a distance away whose clientele was only African women from Ethiopia.

On the day of the test, the models came in one after another, dressed in their native garb with head covering. When the businessman who had put the deal together saw African women flowing in, he shouted, "No more Black people! No more Black people!" About twenty women showed up, many with their children. The first phase of the test had been carried out.

Callie and Pierre did not know that men were not allowed to enter the salon; so, a group of men gathered outside of the salon and sent a woman in to figure out what was going on inside. The salon owner who rented her establishment for the test market explained to the woman what was taking place. And after the woman related that information to the group of men outside, they left the area. Leaving did not help Callie's nerves.

The culture in Dubai was quite different from other Middle Eastern countries. It was the most westernized of all the Middle Eastern countries. During that entire week that the group was in Dubai, the temperature hovered at one hundred seventeen degrees Fahrenheit. The heat was like the heat you feel in Las Vegas, very dry, scorching heat. Something about the men wearing white and the women wearing black clothing just did not seem fair to Callie. Especially to a girl who grew up in Monroeville, wearing little to hardly any clothes in the summer with temperatures never reaching that degree made Callie feel sad for the women wearing black.

The same high-end stores that existed in the United States existed in Dubai. The sponsors had arranged an evening of fun, where the entire group went on a desert safari. When they got to the desert, Callie wondered how could anyone know where you were going because the desert went on for miles and miles. No houses and no businesses were anywhere in sight. Just cinnamon colored sand and it was beautiful. Callie asked her driver, who was one of about six drivers of dune-buggies in a caravan: "How can you possibly know where you are going?" He pointed to a compass that she had not noticed, which was located right above the rear-view mirror.

The driver was quite professional looking but drove like he was drunk. Maybe that was the thrill of the ride he wanted them to experience. Callie was having a problem with the twists and turns; yet she managed to keep her thoughts to herself. Previously, she had threatened Pierre that she was going to ride a camel if she had to go to Dubai. It may not appear as a threat to you; nonetheless, from her perspective, that was a threat.

Pierre was overly protective of her, and she knew that he would not have wanted her to ride a camel because of the potential for an injury. Outside of that, Pierre would not take her threat seriously because he knew she was afraid of animals and heights. Hence, when they were nearing the end of the desert safari, they saw people riding camels right beside the caravan of dune-buggies when Callie said under her breath, "Wow, they are so big and tall." Pierre heard her, laughed and said, "Um hm." She paid him no mind because she was trying to figure out how she was going to save face.

At the end of their safari, the dune-buggies pulled into a camp which had the camels that Callie had seen earlier. As they were passing by the train of camels, Callie asked the driver, "Would you please stop and unlock the door?" Pierre did not know what Callie was about to do. She said nothing further until she jumped out of the car, ran over to the camel, and sat on it!

Pierre was counting on Callie giving way to her fears. He was yelling, "Callie, Callie, be careful!" When Callie sat on the camel, it was sitting on all four of its legs on the ground. The attendant helped Callie to hold on to the right handles on the saddle. Even with padding on the hump of the camel and the padding on her behind, Callie still hurt like she was sitting upon a pointed object. When the camel got up, it flung her downward like she was making a nosedive into the earth, then the camel flung her backward like she was an arrow aiming for the sky. That may be backwards. But you better believe she was so nervous, she was about to release another bump, one that could hardly allow her back into the caravan with the other people.

Pierre had taken a few photos before she made her escape to the camels. He had taken pictures of goats headed to the cliff in the mountains. Once he did that, he jumped on a camel right behind Callie. They rode the camels in a little circle around the camp. By then, it was dark. Once the ride was finished, they had a lovely Middle Eastern dinner prepared for them while belly dancers performed.

After dinner, Callie was determined to prove to Pierre that she could do anything once, and she went trudging around the camp looking for things to do when she saw a man holding a falcon. She asked if she could hold it. Callie had never done any of these things before or since. Walking further, again out in the middle of nowhere, she saw one young woman, while on a cell phone, painting henna on the legs of a tourist.

As Callie waited in line to have a closer look at the painting, she decided to have the young woman paint her ankles with the henna. Although the lady told Callie that the henna would only last a few weeks, it lasted Callie about six weeks, even though she scrubbed her legs every day.

As soon as the evening of entertainment ended, they went back to their hotel totally drained. Pierre had a goal that he kept no matter what, reading a chapter from the Bible daily. He came to the point in the passage which read, "Who set the time for the mountain goats to enter the cliff?" Pierre tried to explain to Callie what he witnessed shortly before he got on the camel saying, "The goats were running like someone was pushing them or running after them and as the last one got into the mountain cliff, the sun went down! I saw that with my very own eyes!"

"Huh?" Callie said. Well, it would have taken a miracle for Callie to understand what he was saying with all her activity during that time. Pierre told all his friends when he returned to Atlanta about his experience concerning the goats running into the crag.

Callie and Pierre had done everything that they were contracted to do. The representatives for the investor were impressed; therefore they made their report to the investor and the results were finally in. Part two of the project would be held in Atlanta. If this deal were sealed in Atlanta, things would really change for them financially.

Now, they were back in Atlanta and the big day had arrived. Everything was arranged beautifully for the presentation. They had only used a small part of the money they had earned from the Dubai test to set up the next phase in Atlanta. Fortunately, they would not have the same challenges they had in Dubai, since they would not have to test the product again. Their goal in Atlanta was only to meet the investor, introduce their team and work out the numbers.

Earlier, they collaborated with the investor's representatives concerning the details for the meeting. They would have a working lunch, since the investor had other engagements. They reserved an entire restaurant. Pierre, Callie and their team met the investor from Dubai. Lunch was served, and everything was going quite well. Toward the end of the meal, Pierre began the presentation. The investor received a call in the middle of the presentation and apologized to Pierre, saying that he needed to take the call.

Once he finished speaking on the telephone for just a few minutes, he said that he received information concerning another business venture and he was going to pursue that instead of this project. The only information they could get from his representatives was that it was a perfume line. Just like that, he changed his mind. He was off to another business enterprise. Everyone's emotions went through the stratosphere.

The investor had flown across the world for a two-hour luncheon meeting that turned into a thirty-minute luncheon, and he never finished his meal. More pain was inflicted when the couple's brand-new camcorder that the two had bought for the presentation was stolen by one of the parking lot attendants at the restaurant. Callie played this tune with the lyrics, "She Couldn't Spell Debt." It had now become her emotional anthem.

Since they had gone to Dubai, the couple's friends thought things had changed for them financially. Friends asked, "Who goes to Dubai for business?" By now the couple knew they would be driving a Ford. Callie and Pierre put their game face on while laughing and conducting themselves as usual; though, they were facing their biggest financial humiliation, not being able to pay for their house. You see, it was one thing not to be able to pay for extras or a car for that matter, but your home?

Nevertheless, this is the positive viewpoint they searched for and found. They were disappointed; but not bitter. They felt alone at times; but not lonely because they had each other. They were embarrassed, but hospitable through it all. They worked to build up others when they themselves were down. They developed an appreciation of giving because of not consistently having. They found strength in the constant battle of fighting debt, and they endured.

They were getting calls every day from the mortgage company, or at least it seemed that way. The countdown was on. Pierre spoke with a loan officer who said that he could help the couple keep their home. He suggested what Pierre could do and it boiled down to lying. At that moment, Pierre said to Callie, "I know I am not a perfect person. At least, there is no way I would agree to do something underhanded to hold on to a house that we clearly knew we could not afford from the beginning. We were too ambitious, and we did not count the cost. We figured it would all work out. And some things just do not work out."

Ignoring questionable motives by the independent mortgage broker got them into the house. Callie knew her husband was right. At this point, the house did not belong to them. It never did. Even if they had paid it off, they were going to be taxed yearly on the property. And if they were unable to pay their taxes, they could lose their house because of a tax debt.

Shortly thereafter, their realtor mentioned that he had a prospective buyer. The buyer was one of Pierre's fraternity brothers from college. He came by one Saturday to view the house with his girlfriend. Callie was in the master bedroom and did not see the need to exit the bedroom for their viewing. Over one hundred people had toured their home. One more would not make Callie get up. Little did Callie know that he would be the one.

The devastated duo had to get this completed quickly, being that foreclosure was right around the corner. Callie thought it would go just as smoothly as it did when they bought the house; however, it did not happen like that. It was one thing or another. Once it was some document that they needed. Then, it was the buyer trying to get money that was tied up somewhere else. You will not believe this one. What was the exact address of the house? Murphy's law was in full force.

There was an error in the street name recorded. Callie labored endlessly trying to get it corrected when they first bought the house. She called the closing attorney's office so many times; yet she was ignored. She documented each telephone conversation. In a bizarre sense, her endless hours of trying to do the right thing by correcting the address, not excluding, being given the runaround by the attorney's office was starting to pay off. It took some months longer for the bank to foreclose on them since their address was recorded incorrectly.

It seemed like they had everything in the palms of their hands. With the delayed foreclosure, still the fraternity brother was unable to pull everything together, thus; their house was sold on the courthouse steps, the same courthouse where Callie and Pierre were married. The realtor, who they thought was a friend, turned on the couple and became self-righteous, spreading gossip to the couple's friends that Callie and Pierre were squatters. Untrue! They were prepared to leave before the final decree was issued.

Incredibly though, Callie was concerned if the realtor would get paid for the work he had done. He never called to check on them or say, "Thank you for your business." He never related what happened to the house after they left. She did not know how a foreclosure worked. They found out from Pierre's frat brother who bought the house at the price that was negotiated before foreclosure.

Eventually, Callie ran into the realtor at the Bank and asked, "Did you ever get paid for your work?" He answered, "Yes." No further comments, no thank you for your business and no inquiry of how they made out. Was that too much to ask? Obviously so, since Callie was hoping he would rally around them like her other friends did when she misspelled debt in the fourth-grade spelling bee. He could not have been a devoted friend!

He forgot that Callie selected him who she felt was a friend. No doubt, he forgot how they stuck with him even though Callie and Pierre's next-door neighbor, who was a realtor, had informed them that the reason their house had not sold was because the agent did not advertise in key places. They shared that information with him so that he could correct the situation.

Was he holding a grudge about that? Perhaps when they did not vacate the house after he learned that it was a clerical error that extended the foreclosure process, his role switched to judge. Even if his misguided feelings drove him to think negatively about them, he forgot his professional manners. A simple courtesy of saying any of these expressions would have been gracious. "Thank you for your business or I am very sorry things did not work out for you as we had hoped a year ago or Thank you for choosing me."

This was a critical turning point for Callie. She needed to feel something good came out of the deal at least for her fair-weather friend. To excuse his behavior, Callie reminded herself that we all make mistakes and she certainly had made her share of mistakes.

She tried her best to appreciate what God had done for her by allowing her to have a beautiful home, husband and good friends. And she especially tried to remember what her good friends had done for her. Then after everything was said and done, Callie found out the true reason for her so-called friend's behavior. His wife had left him for a younger man. Not only that, his wife took all the furniture out of their seven thousand square foot house, while he was out of the country.

Chapter 13: A Friend Believed

From time to time, Callie researched debt because her conscience kept accusing her. She read articles, listened to financial advisers who gave advice and within years changed their position on the advice given. That was confusing for her, and she did not know who or what to believe. What God thought about debt and bankruptcy was important to Callie.

He could read her heart and decide if she deserved mercy. She wanted to live as a Christian. And yet, Callie already knew not paying debts owed was not kin to being a Christian. Even if you did not believe in the Bible, it just made sense we are supposed to pay back whatever we borrowed. Callie realized that at an early age. She certainly was not a criminal nor interested in becoming one. Was she simply a by-product of her inexperience or imperfection?

Here is what she learned from examining the Bible book named Proverbs: "The rich rules over those of little means and the borrower is servant to the man doing the lending." Callie learned that she did not like the feeling of being a servant to the person lending. She learned more.

A person may not make a payment because something unexpected occurred, something tragic like an accident or a death of a family member. That's just a reality in life. Sometimes creditors may pressure debtors and the only way that debtors can protect themselves is through bankruptcy, which the law allows for their protection. The principle came from the Old Testament or Hebrew Scriptures, as some say.

On the flip side, a person might be in debt because of simply not using self-control or because of not using reasonable foresight in all financial decisions. Callie believed that financial irresponsibility was a problem that should be avoided. Knowing the Golden Rule which goes like this,

"Treat others as you would like others to treat you" made Callie sad because she was unable to live up to it, especially in financial matters. Truth be told, we should be exemplary in all seriousness to meet our financial obligations.

Callie's husband asked her why she never, ever wanted to call a bill collector to make payment arrangements. He noticed that she would make every excuse possible. She was nervous about anything that had to do with financial matters, whether she had to call a bill collector or call the bank for the balance. He thought that calling the bank should have been a daily duty for her.

She felt extremely uncomfortable when talking with a customer service representative at a bank. Pierre would ask, "Did you call the bank or get the balance today?" Callie was nervous when he asked that question. She would start talking about anything and everything, just as if she did not hear him or understand the question. He would say, "Please, just answer the question." "No." He asked another question: "Why not?" She did not want to answer that question either. Pierre explained, "Anybody can take money out of the account. It is better to check it out every day. That is not a lot of time nor a big task Callie." Furthermore, Callie got nervous when she wrote a large dollar amount on a check, even though, she knew that they had the money in the bank account.

On several occasions after logging into her online banking account, Callie found herself holding her breath, until she saw the balance. She looked at the computer screen like she was anticipating a person was going to pop out any minute and say, "Look, you overdrew your account! You will have to pay for that!"

Many times, when Callie checked their bank account and it was negative, she felt like she was having an allergic reaction. She started swelling like something had stung her and by the end of the week the swelling was noticeable, in the form of weight gain. Her weight and her debt yo-yoed. When her debt was out of control, her weight was too. When her debt was under control, her weight was too.

Everything around Callie and Pierre had collapsed. They were now out of the house. No car, no business and bankrupt. Pierre got a job as an overnight manager for a five-star hotel before the negative information posted to the credit bureau. Callie found a job as a receptionist. They moved into a little efficiency apartment in downtown Atlanta where they started all over again. Their positive disposition had changed temporarily, and they strained to get their morale up. Then a glimmer of hope surfaced.

Not long into their stay at their little efficiency, they received a call from the Internal Revenue Service. At this point, they had nothing to lose. They invited the agent to their little efficiency apartment for a meeting. She was very kind and not intimidating but listened attentively to what they shared with her. Callie called the Internal Revenue Service several times later after the agent's meeting with them. She tried hard to find her; to their disappointment, they were not able to find her again. They wanted to thank her for the little massage of kindness that she expressed as they needed it desperately.

Callie hoped that one day soon things would change for them just as it had occurred for them in the past. This time was different because this was just not a small financial reversal. This was a total devastation. For Callie to keep her hope alive about every day, she would take color swatches with her to work and ask her co-workers what they thought about this color or that color. Finally, one of them asked

Callie if she were redecorating her house. Callie responded, "No, not yet." He then asked another question. "Are you buying a new house?" Callie responded, "No, not right now." And he asked yet another question. "Then, why are you looking at color swatches?" Callie responded, "It's for when I get a new home." He said, "That doesn't make sense. How do you know which colors to put where without looking at the walls or the house?" Callie told him, "That doesn't matter to me. I know what furniture I own." That little exercise kept Callie busy and hopeful.

She was experiencing extreme exhaustion when she booked an appointment with her Doctor. The doctor thought a thyroid problem or chronic fatigue syndrome. She wrote an order for Callie to get an ultrasound. Nothing was wrong with her thyroid and further testing revealed that there was no reason for her extreme exhaustion. Her doctor asked if anything in Callie's life was causing her stress. Callie told her, "No, we had some challenges earlier; now, we are better." As they talked more, the doctor realized that they had gone through such a big ordeal. The doctor admitted that she could not fathom going through what they had gone through. She said, "It is a wonder you all did not try to commit suicide." Callie told her, "That never entered into our minds. When you have your heart tied to riches as some people do, suicide may seem like the only source of relief. Not in my community. As poor people, we recognize that setbacks can be an everyday occurrence. We have learned that we can start over."

About seven months had passed. They were barely keeping up with their basic needs and in conjunction with that they were wondering when things would change. Some of their friends would call to check on them, trying to reassure the couple in their devastation. Then one day, the lady who taught Callie a lot about the Bible and who had a terrific sense of humor phoned her. Darling is what she often called Callie.

This day was the same. She said, "Darling, I heard that you and Pierre are homeless." Callie said, "Yeah I heard that too." She went on to say, "You know I lease apartments. I also have a few condos I lease. I have one if you would like to look at it." Callie replied, "I don't know." Her friend said, "After you check with Pierre and before you make up your mind, go by and look at it. I will leave the key under the mat." Callie said, "Okay." She gave Callie directions to the property and what do you know, Callie was familiar with the area, and she did not waste any time calling Pierre to tell him about it.

Pierre was at work on his night shift; hence, he asked Callie to go look at it. He said, "Just watch yourself. Be careful." She drove to the condo without a problem, looked under the mat and found the key. When she entered, it looked very basic. It was three-bedrooms, two and a half bathrooms, kitchen, living room with a fireplace and a patio. The interesting thing about the property is that it was one-fourth of a mile from where Callie used to work and about three miles from her house that the couple lost.

Early in their marriage when Pierre and Callie were sharing one car, he would drop Callie off at work and pick her up from work. As they passed this subdivision, Pierre would turn on his signal light to turn left so he could see the pond. Callie would say, "No not today. I am tired. Let's go home." He would say, "We are just driving by. It won't take long. I just wanted to look at the pond again." Callie would say, "Why look at it. We can't afford it." At that time, the subdivision was about two years old. This is where Callie's friend sent her.

From childhood, Callie had chosen this attitude of being indifferent to protect herself in case something did not work out the way she had hoped it would. So, she employed this coping mechanism of being indifferent as soon as she spoke with Pierre about the condo. Callie's humdrum response was, "It's okay. With our furniture, a little paint, change a few fixtures, it would be okay." She did not want him to get overly excited just in case things did not work out. It backfired because the first thing Pierre asked Callie when she picked him up from work was to drive to the condo. Before they went inside, they sat in their car looking at the corner condo unit when they saw three little white-tailed rabbits in the yard at peace.

Now, that they had seen this, they needed to know what was the cost of leasing the condo. The next day after Pierre got some rest, they went to get a bite to eat and during their meal, they discussed what they would say to their friend. And I am sure you know that Callie wanted Pierre to call. Although Pierre did not mind doing it, he thought it would be proper for Callie to call since she had a closer relationship with her. She was old enough to be Callie's grandmomma; therefore, Callie wanted to say the right thing and not offend her. It took a lot of time before Callie would finally make the call.

Her friend asked, "Callie darling, what did you think about the condo?" Callie was not enthusiastic when she said, "It was okay." She asked, "Has Pierre seen it?" Callie said, "Yes, but he was concerned about the cost." Callie then asked her, "How much is it per month?" She told Callie, "It is one thousand three hundred and fifty dollars per month." That was more than they could afford. Callie asked, "Is there a deposit?" She said, "Six hundred and fifty dollars." Needing time to think, Callie asked her, "Can you give me a little time to pass this on to Pierre? I will give you a call back."

Pierre and Callie discussed it and it would be close. If they decided to take it, there would be no wiggle room financially. Callie called her friend back and communicated what they had discussed. During their telephone conversation, Callie thought of a potential problem that she and Pierre had not considered. They would need to complete a rental application. Callie had to let her friend know the entire truth. She explained, "Our credit has been ruined by the foreclosure and the likely bankruptcy. That

would disqualify us. I don't think it would be a good idea."
The friend listened attentively without interrupting Callie.

When Callie finished her spill, the friend said, "Oh darling, I know you. That's enough for me." Callie choked up and could not finish talking with her. She did not scold Callie or think any less of Callie. Loyally, she showed pure confidence in her friend. As Callie wiped her eyes and cleared her throat, she whimpered, "Thank you."

Can you believe it? She dismissed the fact that Callie was a credit risk, that Callie had lost everything. She proved to be a loyal friend. When they gave the friend the six hundred- and fifty-dollars' deposit, it was in three or four supermarket money orders. They all laughed. The friend had the contract already prepared for the three of them to sign. She allowed Callie to attach an addendum, which included that they could paint, hang pictures, and change light fixtures.

Once they moved in, her friend made sure that if anything were remotely uncomfortable, she would handle it. Callie reminded her friend of their allergies. Her friend had a company come out and clean the entire ventilation system.

The friend's husband changed the closets by adding several types of racks and the last thing that her friend did was change the locks on the front door. Callie bought paint, light switches and miscellaneous items from Home Depot that cost about two hundred dollars spread out over the course of about three months. They now had a home.

The friend eventually retired, and a new agent took her place. He treated them with the same care that the friend did. A couple of years had passed since they moved into the condo and now the devastated duo was delighted, settled in and ready to revisit the lawsuit they filed when their contract was illegally taken from them. It had not reached the statute of limitations, which was six years.

Callie called many attorneys for representation. When she met with them and they saw the data, they would eventually decline representation. Another one of Pierre's college friends spoke with Pierre and said that if he ever were in a lawsuit, he would get this attorney to represent him. They asked him why. He said, "This attorney won a lawsuit filed against my investment firm." They thought that was hilarious.

They followed his recommendation and contacted the attorney by telephone. He asked them to send some basic information about the case for his review via fax. They told him that they were not able to pay for any legal fees upfront and they wondered if he would take the case on a contingency basis. He agreed to meet with them and asked them to bring all their files on the case for his examination. They did. He also asked how they heard about him. Pierre told him the story that his friend related. The attorney remembered the case.

This attorney assured them that that they would not incur any debt on this case. He would contact them after he had reviewed everything. Time passed, and he set up another meeting with the husband-and-wife team. He commended them for keeping excellent records and said it was very easy to follow. He felt that they had a case that he could win; hence, taking the case would not be a problem.

He warned them about the disruption to their life that this lawsuit could bring. He knew from their conversation with him that they had already suffered a great deal and were rebuilding their lives. He just wanted them to think about this lawsuit seriously. He wanted them to know that it would be a battle and that the case could go on for at least three years. He said that these people, referring to the manufacturing company, fight hard and that not only would the couple be affected adversely, their friends and families would be affected also. Summing it up, he said, "This Company is relentless."

The attorney ran the numbers based upon the three-year projection for the case. Seeing their earlier sales goals within a six-month period, the lawsuit would be for that amount, about five hundred thousand dollars. They would only receive about eighty thousand dollars after the attorney fees were deducted.

Bottom line was his fee would be upwards of four hundred thousand dollars if the case did not settle quickly. For this firm to wait three years for payment, said to them that they unequivocally would win. Pierre and Callie needed to meditate deeply on whether they should take another risk or let go.

They thanked the attorney for his advice and informed him that they would make their decision and follow-up the next day.

They all met the next day and Pierre said, "We considered the fight. Bringing our friends and family into our problem is not a consideration. We decided not to pursue the lawsuit against this manufacturer. We believe that we could make more than eighty thousand dollars between the two of us in three years without all the harassment heaped upon us and our families. Although, it may not take that long, we cannot afford to tie up our lives anymore, even if it is only six months. Furthermore, we would have to work the next three years at least while the case was being litigated."

The attorney seemed to be proud of their decision when he said, "You made the right choice. I have no doubt that my firm would have won. You two seem like nice people and I am sorry that this happened to you. Please keep me in mind if you need help in the future." They thanked the attorney again for his advice. They promised that they would use his services if they had a need in the future. He did not charge the couple one dime and Pierre's friend could not believe it.

Knowing that they did not want to be tempted to reverse their decision, they had a bonfire to destroy the files once and for all. It was over. Along with their decision, the manufacturer dropped their countersuit against them for slander. Initially, the couple really wanted to wage warfare against this company because they had destroyed their lives. Callie's disposition changed. She did not want any more conflict.

Like her great granddaddy would suffer a monetary loss to avoid conflict, Callie would, too. In all situations, it is smarter to count the cost, emotionally and financially for sure. They could have continued with the lawsuit and won just to prove a point. Perhaps, the case would not have taken three years. Even another year added to what they had previously experienced could have created stress with potent health problems. After their decision, Pierre and Callie never said to each other, what if.

Chapter 14: Upgraded

Catastrophe

Pierre was still sensitive about Callie going back to work full-time after they had lost everything. He took pride in caring for her and he felt that it was an assault against his manhood. He already knew Callie was always the type of person who wanted to contribute. This was no different. She would make the best of an unpleasant situation, find full-time employment and make some money. How could she do it without offending her husband?

This is how Callie went about doing it. During football season, Pierre was watching the game and was very much into it when Callie slipped into the bedroom to look for jobs on the computer. Within a few minutes he yelled, "What are you doing?" Callie responded, "Reading the paper." He said, "What paper?" Callie said, "The paper on the computer, The AJC. A few more minutes passed. Instead of yelling from the living room, this time, he just opened the door to the bedroom and asked, "What are you doing?" Callie jumped. "Nothing! Just reading the paper." She tried to close the screen when he asked, "Why did you do that?"

His mannerisms suggested that he was suspicious of her response. Callie finally admitted that she was looking for a job. He said, "Don't I provide for you? Why do you want to look for a job?" Callie said, "Yes. You have taken loving care of me to the best of your ability." After a quick silent prayer, Callie came back with this response. "It's important for me to have a check written in my name. It just makes me feel better about me." She could tell that Pierre had not thought about that angle and besides that, she dignified him. She showed him that it was much more than what he was doing or not doing. It involved something that she needed to work for, her self-esteem.

Callie was very excited about one of the jobs she had applied for, and she felt confident that she would get it. Pierre asked Callie every day for about a month, "Did you get a response? Callie would say to him, "Give it another week. You'll see." She was embracing positive thinking and it worked. She interviewed and was offered the position. She accepted the secretarial position with a salary of twenty-four thousand dollars per year. Callie loved the job and the people; except, she hated the expense associated with her new job.

At first glance, having a job seemed beneficial. She had not considered the clothes she needed to buy, dry cleaning, gas for her car as well as parking, especially on such a low salary. Other than that, she had cash-flow and a check written in her name. You can tell her self-esteem was increasing because she began to walk differently, purposefully and with confidence. After being in her job about six months, Callie started feeling better about herself.

She applied for another job within the company, which doubled her salary. Within a year Callie was earning fifty-five thousand dollars per year. She stayed in that job for four years. She gave her husband thirty thousand dollars from the money she had saved to restart his business. In one weekend, he grossed sixty-seven thousand dollars at a trade show which helped them with re-establishing their home and business. They both were feeling pretty good again.

In late August, Pierre and Callie were invited to a wedding in Louisiana. A dear friend of her husband asked them to stop in New Orleans to see the house that he had renovated for his parents. Since Pierre's friend and his wife were invited to the wedding in Louisiana, they all had planned to ride together. Callie had taken two days off from work, the Friday before the wedding and Monday after the wedding to make it a nice long weekend.

Pierre's friend picked them up from their hotel in New Orleans and brought them to his parents newly renovated home. After taking the tour of the home, they went to a nice restaurant for dinner. While sitting in the restaurant, Callie noticed a woman at a nearby table who had a delicious-looking drink, which was presented in a glass that looked like a mini punch bowl. She asked the lady what was the name of the drink. The lady responded, "It is a Hurricane." When the waiter took their drink orders, Callie said, "I want a Hurricane." Everyone at the table laughed because it was the biggest drink at the table.

Callie ordered the Hurricane, not knowing that like debt, the Hurricane would chase her. After sipping the drink, her facial expression said, "Life is good." The food was simply wonderful. Because the wedding was the next day, they decided to end their evening a little early.

On their way to the hotel, Pierre's friend mentioned that there was news of a Hurricane coming through New Orleans. Pierre and Callie had not heard about it. By the time they entered their hotel room, they had forgotten his comment. Instead of turning on the television to get an update, they began rehashing their entire evening with each other and then went to bed.

Saturday morning, Pierre got up early to get breakfast for them both. Callie started to leisurely prepare for the wedding by styling her hair first. Just before she had finished getting dressed, Pierre's friend telephoned them and informed them that the Hurricane was coming their way, and that he and his wife were preparing to get his elderly parents out of town. Callie recognized this Hurricane was not the one she could drink and enjoy. She and Pierre had flown into New Orleans; therefore, she was puzzled as to how they would get to the wedding. She could not understand why her husband was not as concerned as she was.

When she contacted another uncle, who lived in New Orleans, she got no answer to her telephone calls. Undoubtedly, all of them had gone to a safer location. The couple decided to watch the news for updates on the hurricane. They discovered that the Mayor of New Orleans was asking for a voluntary evacuation from the city which later escalated to a mandatory evacuation.

The Hurricane was expected to be at a level five which would be life threatening to the couple and bring major devastation to the city's structure. What would they do? Pierre would speak with the groom to inform him of what had occurred and that they would be unable to attend the wedding.

Their next goal was to get out of New Orleans, especially since the Hurricane was targeted to hit downtown, where they were staying. They tried to get an earlier flight to Atlanta; except, flights had been cancelled. They tried to get a rental car; but then again, no cars were available. They called Amtrak train system. No trains were running. They called Greyhound Bus line. As Callie was speaking to the customer service agent, the agent announced to Callie that all bus schedules had just been cancelled. Finally, Pierre went walking down the street to find a horse and buggy. Much to their dismay, nothing was available. There was no way out.

Pierre was calm. Callie was in a state of panic. Now she really wanted a Hurricane to calm her nerves. Her emotions went from disappointment of not getting a chance to attend the wedding to being angry that her friends left her in New Orleans, stuck downtown as a target, bulls-eye for the Hurricane.

On Sunday, the hotel staff informed everyone that the hotel would be functioning as a shelter and not as a hotel. Additionally, Management gave everyone instructions on how to prepare for the Hurricane. One directive included filling each bathtub and basin with water. They were to place their luggage in the bathroom, assemble on another floor when notified, and bring the flashlight that each person was given. The thought of drinking water from the bathtub motivated Callie to clean it extremely well. While Callie was cleaning the tub, Pierre took his rest.

All night long, Callie prepared as they had been instructed. This was to a fault because she did not get any rest. She had not slept since Saturday night, and it was now five a.m. Monday morning. She could hear the pressure of the wind shaking the hotel windows; still, that did not cause Pierre to wake up. She decided to take a walk. She sat with an employee who was guarding the elevator. Shortly thereafter, Pierre ran around the corner. I guess he thought Callie had left him. He encouraged her to try to get some sleep. They returned to their hotel room and within fifteen minutes, it was time to change their location to the hallway between the elevators.

There they sat on the floor, with just a pillow, from about five forty-five a.m. to about two-thirty p.m. It was cramped and uncomfortable with about thirty people in that small space. One man who sat beside Callie snored like he had swallowed a cocktail of different sounds, ranging from the sound of a growling bear to the whishing sound of a whale to a baby's gentle hum. Out of all the people there, why did this man have to sit beside her, then eventually lie down beside her?

After the Hurricane had passed through, the hotel staff completed their walk-through, and all could return to their rooms. There was no power, no running water, plus their food was limited. City residents who came to the hotel for refuge had brought their food with them. Tourists did not have that advantage. Many had not eaten since Sunday. Therefore, on Monday about six p.m., they left the fourteenth floor to walk to the seventh floor for a half ham sandwich and a small cup of water, the size of a cup you would use to gargle after brushing your teeth.

Those who had obeyed the instruction to fill the bathtub with water were truly pleased to have complied. Others, who had not, would have to travel to the seventh floor to get water from the swimming pool to flush their toilets and to clean their bodies. Carrying the water from the seventh floor to various floors by the stairwell caused many spills, which in turn, caused several accidents. Callie wanted to help Pierre who helped many that were disabled. But in fact, Callie was just not strong enough because she was sleep deprived. Still though, they felt some relief because they had made it through the Hurricane. The next day brought more anxiety. The levies broke. Water was filling the city.

It was very hot in New Orleans. In fact, it was scorching hot. There was hardly any wind blowing. The couple stripped down to their underwear as they went out to the patio connected to the hotel room to get some air and they could not feel any breeze. The only light that was illuminating the sky came from helicopters flying over the city with flood lights beaming down and around. And each time a helicopter passed by, Callie dashed into the room; so, the helicopter driver could not see her. On one of her quick runs to their room, she hit her foot so hard that she thought she had broken it.

Tuesday morning, they went to the seventh floor to get something to eat. Callie was excited when she heard others say that they were having biscuits. She imagined having a large buttermilk biscuit with blackstrap molasses. The excitement did not last long after she picked up the biscuit from the table. It was hard as a rock and Callie could not bring herself to eat the biscuit nor throw it away. She wrapped it in a napkin to save for later just in case they were unable to get any more food.

Each person picked up about four ounces of orange juice, which Callie gave to her husband because she hated orange juice. She had bought water at a supermarket to bring to the hotel because water was quite expensive at hotels. This time was no different. Callie had bought a gallon of water when they first made it to New Orleans and now that was gone. She was getting sick. She could not bring herself to drink the water from the bathtub. Subsequently, she had nothing to drink.

The hotel manager asked Pierre if he could help them since Pierre had volunteered the day before. He gladly accepted on one condition, that the manager would give Callie some water to drink. The manager gave her a pitcher of water from the kitchen. When Callie got the water, four to five people asked for some. She had one glass and shared the rest with others.

The hotel's management asked Pierre to help move some of the handicapped people to lower floors and to go to the nearby Walgreens to secure snacks and water for the people. Pierre was happy to help. He saw looting in the city. The manager of the Walgreens did something unusual. He opened the front door so that people could come in to get whatever food and drink they needed. The manager said this, "What I don't understand is why are people taking items that they cannot use now? Food and water should be at the top of the list. They are taking everything except food."

Pierre brought back melted ice cream, soft M&M candy without nuts, potato chips, soft drinks and Gatorade. Callie was allergic to milk. Yes, the ice cream, with the consistency of a milk shake was what Callie would consume. She rarely drank soft drinks. Yet, Callie ate all the things that he brought back.

Another one of Pierre's tasks was to siphon gasoline from the cars, so that the hotel could use the back-up generator. Pierre was an excellent negotiator. He said, "If I do that; then, I will need to charge my cell phone on the generator to keep in contact with our friends." Callie was protective and fearful for her husband. She was especially concerned about all the unknown chemicals and trash in the water in the streets. Pierre did not have the proper shoes on, and his feet were turning yellow. Finally, the hotel manager gave Pierre a work uniform with boots.

Once Pierre fully charged his mobile phone, he left a greeting on the cell phone that included updates on their situation. In the meantime, the newlyweds had just left a voicemail message saying that they were on their way to get Callie and Pierre. When Pierre got the message, he started gathering their luggage to leave.

Callie said, "Pierre, where are you going? We should wait until they get closer. We don't know what they may encounter." He listened to her because it made sense. The couple who had just gotten married, who had called an hour earlier, later called and informed Pierre that the National Guard had taken control of the city. No one could enter.

Pierre went out again to find something that would soothe Callie's upset stomach. He saw a vendor on the street selling rice, a scoop for ten dollars. He stood in line for a long time. The line was so long that he eventually just left. Tuesday morning breakfast was no doubt a bummer. All in line tried to think positive by expecting that Tuesday evening dinner would be much better. Individuals received one half cup of beans and one-half cup of water. Callie was hoping it was not from the bathtub. Pierre smelled something other than beans and followed the smell, leading him to a makeshift kitchen with other hotel staff preparing Jambalaya.

He approached some of the employees who had prepared the Jambalaya and asked if he could have some of the dish because he was starving. They gave him a scoop. Of course, that was not enough for him since he had been working so hard trying to find food, water, and gasoline. On top of that, the staff didn't even ask if Callie wanted to look at it, let alone taste it. Pierre said, "Callie, they are taking care of their own." After that, Pierre and Callie left to go to their room.

By now all the tourists and residents had been asked by hotel management to leave the hotel and go to the Superdome, several blocks from where they were located. While that was occurring, Pierre was at the Walgreens trying to get some water. The hotel manager asked Callie, "Why are you still here?" Callie whispered, "My husband has gone to Walgreens." He said, "You should leave at once." Then Callie asked him, "How can you ask me to leave when you asked my husband to go to Walgreens for water and anything else that the people could use?"

271

He ignored her question and was adamant about Callie getting her belongings and leaving the hotel. She had to think quickly because not only was he unreasonable, he was also unappreciative of all the good suggestions Pierre had given him, which worked out perfectly. Giving him the opportunity to show compassion, Callie whispered, "My husband has the key to the room." The manager instructed another employee to give Callie the master key for the hotel room. When Callie got to her room unescorted, she did not leave her room. She waited for her husband.

When her husband returned, she was crying, trying to explain through the tears what had taken place. He tried to get her to stop crying. Callie was on the brink of a nervous breakdown. With a warm embrace, he said, "Don't cry Callie. Everything is going to be ok. Our Almighty God Jehovah will protect us." Callie was really trying to calm down. But she could not stop shaking. Pierre said, "Look at it like this Callie. God is just training us. We will now be in a better position to help others. You see?"

While wiping her tears with his hands, she asked in frustration, "Can God please train someone else?" They did not leave the hotel that day. They slept in the totally abandoned hotel overnight with the remaining employees.

The following morning Callie was sitting on the couch on the seventh floor and numb. They had their two small bags of luggage and on their way to the Superdome. Suddenly, Pierre asked the general manager of the hotel, "Who does that red flatbed truck in the parking lot belong to?" The manager said, "It belongs to the hotel." You will not believe what Pierre asked next. "Can I drive the flatbed to Baton Rouge to take the employees?" Pierre learned that only two employees had their driver's license and one had left it at home.

Pierre asked Callie to rush back to the hotel room and get a few pillows. In the meantime, he had saved a space for Callie on the flatbed. Her seat would be on their suitcases with a couple of pillows for support. By the time Callie gathered the pillows from the hotel, there was hardly any room for her. She stood on the back of the flatbed leaning against her luggage for the entire trip of four hours to Baton Rouge.

Pierre acted as if he had been a contestant on one of the survivors shows. He kept a profound sense of humor despite everything that had materialized. When he saw the lady that served him one small scoop of Jambalaya, he said in a New Orleans or Geechee accent, "Heeey, how's yo momma and dem? If ya hada known that I wuz da one gonna give ya ah ride, you'da given me a lil mo of that deah Jambalaya. Wouldn't ya know? Yawl gave me that small scoop of Jambalaya and didn't even geah my wife any, cause ya sey, she didn't do nething." He laughed, and they began to laugh.

Then the employees told Pierre how management had left not long ago on the hotel shuttle without trying to take care of them. They said, "They took all dem white people and left us." Pierre's heart went out to them. He said, "Well I got you now. I'm gonna take care of you." Pierre and the other Spanish employee driver, named Alejandro, were the only adult males of which the rest were women and children. Since the male employee did not know how to get to Baton Rouge, here was another shocker. Pierre would lead the two-vehicle caravan of hotel employees to Baton Rouge where he had never been either.

When they came out of the hotel, which was Callie's first visit outside since the hurricane had occurred, she was mesmerized. It looked as if there had been a war. They traveled at a turtle's pace in the flatbed. The water was high, and Pierre maneuvered his way through the water with the help of the National Guard while avoiding the area where others were traveling in canoes.

They missed their first turn near the exit that would take them to Baton Rouge and ended up going in the opposite direction of Baton Rouge over a high bridge where hundreds of people were living. Because so many people were on the overpass, Pierre and the other driver had to drive the vehicles very carefully to avoid hitting people that were either resting or walking in the street, giving one couple the opportunity to approach their vehicle to ask for a ride. Callie felt like she was in the middle of a Sci-Fi flick.

She could not contain her tears when the older couple who was at least seventy-five years old approached her and asked, "Is there any room for us? Can we go with you?" That request was imbedded in her brain, and she had drama filled dreams for months.

They were dressed in very light clothing, a t-shirt and shorts and Callie could tell that they were weak physically, like they just needed to lie down for a little while. For some reason Pierre did not see them and Callie was standing up leaning against her suitcases when she said, "There is no room anywhere on the vehicle."

They were packed like sardines in a can. Callie told Pierre later how sad she felt when she told the elderly couple there was no room. She felt worse when Pierre said, "I wish you had gotten my attention and asked me. I would have figured out a way to get them on the flatbed." She knew after he said that he could have done so.

It took about four hours to drive to Baton Rouge, which normally they learned would have taken far less time if the driving conditions had been better. The youngest family sat in the cabin of the flatbed with Pierre, a two-month-old baby, a five-year-old boy and his momma of about twenty-five years old. And naturally the others were either disheartened because they were sitting on an open, unclean vehicle that had been used to discard trash for the hotel or discouraged for the reason they had been left behind by their management team.

As they traveled along the highway, Callie was unaware of how hot the sun was because of the refreshing breeze she felt, until they had almost made it to Baton Rouge. Her husband kept telling her to put a towel on her head. Callie did not want to do that, for she liked feeling the wind since the air was still for days.

Then Callie scratched her neck and she noticed that her fingernails had light brown dirt underneath. She thought to herself, "I have been washing off every day. Why am I so dirty?" They finally saw a gas station where they stopped to take a bathroom break and as Callie stepped off the truck, Pierre said, "Look here. Look in the window." She caught a reflection of herself in the window and realized that she had scratched the skin off her neck and shoulders. She sustained a nasty sunburn.

Right before they stopped at the gas station, there were several men riding alongside them in a car. They were talking to Callie asking, "Do you all need help?" Although that was the first group that had helped, Pierre saw straight through them and recognized that they were up to no good. From the cabin of the flatbed, Pierre yelled to get Callie's attention and he asked her, "Would you please stop talking to them?" When they got to the gas station, a police car was there and the men that had been following them kept going.

After the men did not stop at the convenience store, it was clear that Pierre was correct. Pierre stood at the door of the store waiting for everyone to enter to use the bathroom and he kept that position until everyone came out. After he bought snacks for the children and adults, filled the tank with gas, they continued their journey escorted by the police car that was at the convenient mart.

In Baton Rouge, they were presented with another challenge. The employees could not get a room to rest because there were no rooms, and it was purely chaotic. By now residents from New Orleans had made it to Baton Rouge and were trying to get hotel rooms. Callie knew that Pierre was solution oriented. And so calmly, she tried to explain to the New Orleans hotel employees who had been traveling with them that Pierre would not leave until their arrangements were made. When they saw how lovingly Pierre cared for them, their eyes welled up with tears.

Pierre informed the Baton Rouge hotel staff that this group was their fellow co-workers out of New Orleans. Even though they had no rooms available, he asked if they could please give access to a vacant conference room or ballroom; therefore, they could have a place to rest?

Once the New Orleans employees had access to the ballroom and were safely inside, Pierre then asked the front desk to provide blankets and pillows for that ballroom so that all the employees from New Orleans could have someplace to sleep. It took a little time to get those blankets and pillows; then, they got them.

The next challenge was that none of the employees from New Orleans had eaten anything much or had money to buy anything to eat. Callie did not know where Pierre had gone. She knew that he was doing something constructive. Within about fifteen minutes, Pierre returned with food that he had bought from McDonald's for everyone.

As soon as Pierre had done that, the bride's parents, who lived in Baton Rouge, came to pick Pierre and Callie up. When Pierre told those New Orleans employees that they were leaving, they grabbed him and hugged him like they were never going to let him go. Their tears were dropping all over him and he was seconds away from breaking down in tears. He wondered who would care for them and keep them encouraged. Would they ever meet again?

Since the bride's parents had no air conditioning at their home because of a power outage in that area, they took Callie and Pierre to the home of one of their friends. The homeowner asked, "Were you scared?" Callie said, "Yes, I was." She did not bother to elaborate or inquire why he had asked that question. She was preoccupied to the point of not being able to sleep; even though, the family was very accommodating. Every break Callie received; she would try very hard to get flight reservations to Atlanta. The husband asked Callie, "Why are you in such a rush? You can stay as long as you would like." Callie said, "We need to go because soon it will be hard to get out of Baton Rouge. It's just a matter of time when everyone in New Orleans will be here." He asked, "Have you been able to sleep?" "No. I have not. I just need to get back to Atlanta. You have relief workers here and I don't want to put an additional burden on your family."

Callie was right. It was incredible how difficult it was to schedule a flight, although for a period, she was on the phone nonstop. When she called and got a rejection for whatever reason, she would hang up and call back. Finally, Callie got a person that would honor their prior reservation without more money. They could leave late Friday.

They made it back to Atlanta. Callie was unable to hold her emotions. It was quite remarkable how two people, husband and wife can go through the same disaster, and one is elated, and the other is traumatized. They received lots of invitations from their friends who wanted to learn what happened to them firsthand. Callie declined every one of their invitations for she was depressed about how she handled the situation. She was trying to deal with her regret. She did not hold Pierre back but encouraged him to go on without her.

Eventually, Callie had to review articles on how to handle post-traumatic stress. She had to take medicine for anxiety for about three months. Several months had passed before she was able to discuss this event without feeling like she would have a nervous breakdown. Although, she had met many unpleasant situations, including having an ongoing incapacitating bout with debt, this tribulation trumped everything. She had never come this close to death.

She was sick when she returned to Atlanta. Her time away from work amounted to about a month. She was diagnosed with a respiratory infection, because of all the nasty stuff in the hotel and in the air that she had inhaled. She was also treated for a bad sunburn. Pierre developed some respiratory problems also. Both recuperated fully and went back to their same day to day activities, but not as the same person.

Callie checked the bank specifically for the hotel stay. She was curious about how the hotel would handle the charges since they were not able to check out and get a receipt. After no charge had hit her account, she contacted the hotel. She called several times and after many unsuccessful attempts to reach someone, she dismissed it. Certainly, after such a prolonged period, Callie concluded that they would not be charged. It was truly a natural disaster that affected the southeast.

A couple of months had passed and so Callie called again. She was finally able to speak with someone who said that there was no record of their stay. She was not satisfied with the response; therefore, she called the corporate office. She was informed that because of the hurricane and the devastation around that time, there will be no charges. That sounded reasonable. At that point, she completely forgot about it.

A little over one year had passed and now Callie learned why her husband told her to check the bank daily. He had always told Callie, "Someone can take money out of the account and that would really mess us up." Nearly, one and a half years after the Hurricane had occurred, her check card was charged for the entire hotel stay, including the days that the hotel was used as a shelter for the residents of New Orleans.

Callie thought that they would have surely given them a few nights free, since Pierre had worked so hard taking care of their employees. And judging by how upset those employees were when management left them to fend for themselves after the hurricane, they would have complained about the situation and reported how Pierre came to their rescue. That was not the case. Fortunately, a friend of the couple who worked in the corporate office corrected the entire financial mess. The deduction from their account hit the week before Christmas. The hotel thought that the couple would not have noticed it. They did. Can you imagine the domino effect that could have arisen if they had other transactions waiting to post to their checking account?

Chapter 15: Possibilities Gave

Hope

Callie needed a major change, so she decided to leave her job to pursue real estate, thinking that it would be fun, give income and use her skill set. Since she was hungry for a listing, she went against what she had been trained to do, making her first listing experience dreadful.

Her client would not give the documents that she asked, but kept giving the excuse, "They are in storage in Texas." Callie believed her when she said she had been supporting two homes and a lot of her things were in storage, which would take a little time to find. Callie should not have listed her house until she received all the needed documents.

About a month or so after she had listed the property, her client still had not given Callie the documents. In the meantime, one of the neighbors called Callie. It was more of a venting conversation for him as he complained about one thing after another, particularly how the client's house was dragging down the value of his house and others in the neighborhood. Callie thanked him for his call and ended the conversation: "I will come out and look at the property."

As promised, Callie went out to look at the property, which was awful. The owner had left logs used for the fireplace and all kind of debris in the front yard and in the back yard. Callie would have needed a bulldozer to push the stuff off the lot. Where did it all come from?

It looked as if the homeowner had allowed a junk dealer to store his junk in the backyard. Callie was not able to reach her client to talk about what needed to be done with the yard. Since, she got the tip from the next-door neighbor, she decided to stop by to introduce herself. He was not at home, so Callie left a note. The neighbor called her to let her know that he was extremely impressed that she paid him a visit. He hoped that Callie could persuade the homeowner to act quickly to clean up the mess.

Callie was traveling quite a bit with her husband on another project; once more, the same neighbor who called Callie earlier, informed her that her sign had been removed and replaced with another agent's sign. When Callie received the news from the neighbor, she followed up with the real estate agent who had replaced her sign with his sign. That was her first and last listing.

After that, Pierre and Callie worked on a project which required them to visit over eighty cities within two years. Being that they had been working so hard, Callie wanted to take Pierre to Hawaii for a vacation. Right after buying the tickets, they realized that it was not the right time for them to travel to Hawaii. They changed the date three times because of that fact.

The last time they set the date for travel, Callie had found a property in Honolulu to rent for the week. The properties that the Honolulu agent handled in Maui were all booked. She was determined to make it happen, so she called the agent every day to see if there were any cancellations. She asked the agent if she could recommend someone else with vacancies in Maui. The agent mentioned that she had a company in mind and would call Callie later. While she was talking to Callie, Callie had a pen in hand and was making notes of the conversation. After waiting a few days for the agent to respond, Callie decided to pursue the lead the agent had mentioned on the telephone. She searched the internet and found them in early December. Now Callie could make the final arrangements for Maui.

When she called the agency in Maui, she informed them that they were staying for one month, hoping to get a great break on pricing. It was peak season, near Christmas time, whale season and they were not giving any breaks. Pierre said, "Let's just reschedule." Callie replied, "Not just yet."

Only two weeks remained before their flights were scheduled to leave. Callie called the agent in Maui every day and eight days before their flight was scheduled to leave, the agent divulged that he had a villa near the construction site of the Ritz Carlton Residences in Kapalua. Callie had no clue where that was or what it was. Then, she asked for more information. He gave it to her along with these comments, "People don't want to see construction or hear hammers when on vacation. So that's all that we have available, one villa." Callie said, "I don't know of many construction sites that work at night; so, I don't think that would interfere with our sleep. That does not matter to us. Just please give me an excellent rate." The rate was so good that Callie accepted it while he was in the middle of the sentence and asked, "How may I pay for it?"

Pierre was concerned about the location, thinking that it was a dive since the rate was so low. When he smelled the fresh air after he got off the plane, he said, "This is home." Callie asked, "What do you mean this is home? You have not seen the villa." He had firmly admitted that Atlanta was where he would live until he died, nothing could compare. They had traveled all around the world, and he made an unsolicited statement that caused Callie to view what he said as a foreign language. She couldn't understand it.

Callie wanted to make sure that he had an enjoyable time. Yet, she knew that they needed to stick to the budget, or they would incur debt. To cut their costs, they agreed to prepare their meals at the villa. They only ate out once in

Maui during their month-long vacation. Also, while they were in Honolulu for one week, they did not eat out and prepared their meals.

They visited rainforests, beaches and Haleakala, a volcano that was over ten thousand feet above sea level with a total circumference of twenty-two miles. At the bottom of the summit, the average temperature in the winter was around seventy-eight degrees.

They followed the direction to carry a light coat, since once they got to the top, they would need it because of the change in temperature. Callie just carried her winter coat that she had brought along from Atlanta. As they neared the top of Haleakala, the weather started to change and by the time they got to the top it was about forty degrees. All this beauty did not cost them anything.

When they returned to Atlanta, Pierre at once began telling their friends that they were moving to Maui in two years. When they asked Callie, she would say, "Is that what he said? Well, okay." As they moved closer to their target date, Callie still showed no emotion. Pierre inquired, "Callie, do you want to go to Maui to live?" Callie said, "Yes, I don't mind. I just want you to know a few things. Yes, I was born in the South in a small country town. And yes, I sound Southern. But then, I am a city girl at heart. I like the city." He said, "That's it?" Callie said, "Yes. That's it."

They had been to Honolulu twice and, so he said, "Well, if you feel like you need a little city, we can go to Honolulu from time to time." Callie said, "Okay, no problem." It was that simple.

Now the two years were up, and they were just about finished packing. Some of their friends had not seen them for a while and called to ask where they had been. Since they had been traveling for the past four years, they were primarily asking what cities had they visited? Pierre and Callie told them that they were visiting friends all over Atlanta to say goodbye. They said, "Goodbye? What do you mean goodbye?" Word spread quickly.

Their planned move appeared to have occurred overnight; nevertheless, Pierre had shared their goal with friends and family about two years earlier. Friends wanted to give them a going away party. Callie did not want to have all the attention. Pierre convinced her that it would be good for all of them to say their goodbyes.

Callie was doing fine until the day of the event. Exhausted from all the details she had to wrap up, the invitation finally came by email the morning of the party. They printed the invitation and prepared to go. It was an unbelievable event! Callie was touched by all the work that was done in their behalf. Someone wrote a song that the entire group sang. Another authored a poem that everyone read and one of the speakers was a little girl.

This little girl was special because she was the recipient of the only baby shower Callie had hosted at her house before it went into foreclosure. And now the baby was twelve years old, telling Pierre and Callie how much she was going to miss them. She did not rush, stutter and was very Southern in her delivery. Her purposeful speech along with her inviting warmth melted Callie's heart.

At that moment, Callie did not focus on the negative problems the couple had experienced. Instead, she was reminded of the love that permeated their home, the parties given and attended, and the friendships developed and kept.

Moreover, not to be underestimated was their growth as individuals. They could now empathize with people with various problems. Their experience in life had run the gamut. They were ready to move to Maui.

Callie made it to Maui the day after their wedding anniversary. Pierre had to tie up a few loose ends. He followed within a few days. In the past, when they visited Maui, Pierre always drove. Callie paid little attention to the route he took. Now, she had to figure it out herself. After she stopped at the airport guard station and asked for directions, the attendant said, "There are only two main roads. You will not have a problem. Just follow this one road all the way out. No problem."

Callie did have a problem because it was raining heavily, and she could hardly see. She was supposed to arrive in Maui earlier in the day; however, her flight was delayed twice before she left Atlanta. She arrived about eleven p.m.

Pierre called while she was driving around the mountain in Kahului to see how she was doing. She explained that the traffic was horrible, and she looked in her rear-view mirror to see what appeared to be an endless line of cars following her. He said, "Pull over, let them pass." Callie said, "No way. I am coming around the mountain and I do not want to pull over. I must go. I need to focus." Callie hung up.

About one half hour from when Callie started, the rain was not as heavy. As she approached the community where they would live, the rain stopped. She saw the store where they had shopped. She knew she was almost home. She ran into the store to get some essential food items and continued to their apartment. It felt like someone was guiding her to the apartment.

Before she brought her groceries and luggage inside, she checked out her newly renovated apartment. After she got everything inside, Callie called Pierre, his momma and her momma to let them know that she had made it safely. By the time Callie finished talking with them, it was about three in the morning. She got in the bed and was awakened about three hours later by the bright sunlight. Callie grabbed her phone and took a picture from her upstairs bedroom of the ocean beneath and that became her screensaver to this day.

The day was simply beautiful. It was a goal that they had achieved together with God's help. Callie turned the television on and watched the visitor's channel for almost the entire day. She had food, water and the beautiful scenery. What more could she ask for? I don't think Callie will ever forget that day.

Over the years, it was obvious that the sometimes devastated, sometimes dynamic couple, was challenged by intermittent debt. It was clear that they kept making countless mistakes of which some were repeated. Since life has not ended, they will probably make a few more mistakes. It's not their desire; but it's a fact.

Certainly, news reports expose how many of the influential are in debt or have severe tax problems. Many of them previously in debt are now in debt again.

Callie started thinking about how organizations, big businesses and government have access to some of the most brilliant minds in the world; and thus far, they have not been able to conquer the world's problems or resolve the issue of debt. Perhaps, the couple did not have access to that type of knowledge. The couple got into debt partly by making poor choices, making unwise decisions, greed, tragedy or other unforeseen occurrences.

These are some of the same reasons government and big businesses go into debt. Basically, the conclusion of the matter concerning debt is whether people or institutions owe hundreds, thousands, or trillions, debt is an enemy to basic living. Callie did not know if the leaders in government and big businesses had felt sick to their stomach like she had when she couldn't pay her bills. What Callie knew was that debt had lingered with them as it had lingered with her. Obviously, these ones had not been able to spell debt either.

On the positive side, having debt helped Callie to become more empathetic, compassionate and humble. Although, she couldn't spell debt when she was in the fourth grade, no doubt about it, Callie was still having problems with it as an adult. She acknowledged that she had no reason to boast about anything. She learned that happiness did not revolve around money or things; nevertheless, true happiness revolves around love for God and love for our neighbor.

She learned that when we make a mistake and we do not learn from the mistake; we are certain to repeat it. We are confronted with the same problems until we find a way to change our behavior. As difficult as it may be, making minor changes leads to making bigger changes. Each day, week, month, year has gotten a tiny bit better for Callie. Certainly, she knows she cannot give up trying to conquer her enemy.

While struggling to spell the word "debt" at nine years old initially proved devastating, by the time Callie was a teenager, it appeared trivial. And by the time she was twenty-four years old, she learned that debt was not trivial, and it deserved her attention. Although, the more Callie tried to release herself from debt, she felt as if she were sinking in quicksand. As she compared debt to having a crippling disease, she came to terms with this point about debt: "There are other things that are worse." Can you really imagine having a physical or psychological debilitating disease? Leukemia or Schizophrenia? Can you imagine losing a loved one in death? Your child? Your husband? Your wife? Or your best friend? Can you imagine going through a natural disaster? Now financial debt seems to be the lesser of other troubles. Yet debt, no matter how hard you try, like a crippling disease, may not go away quickly. Callie worked through debt. So, like a disease that can go into remission if you take the steps to seek treatment and manage it, debt can too.

Callie found comfort through the comments of Miami Herald columnist Leonard Pitts, who stated, "There is value in going through adversity. A person learns that failure is not fatal, and devastation is not eternal. One gains depth. One becomes ready." When Callie struggled hard to do something positive like paying off debt, and was not able to consistently do it, she felt like a failure. Now when Callie is confronted with very difficult financial challenges, instead of feeling like a failure, she asks the question, "Is this fatal?" Once Callie figures out that it is not fatal, then she concludes with the thought, "And this too shall pass."

Consuelo Danita loves to write about subjects that deal with everyday life. ConsueloDanita.com

www.ingramcontent.com/pod-product-compliance
Lightning Source LLC
Chambersburg PA
CBHW021313250626
47155CB00002B/509